I0690376

The Rootless Nomad

The Rootless Nomad

Ségu Séribandi

Abibiman
Publishing

New York & London

First published in the United Kingdom in 2025 by
Abibiman Publishing
www.abibimanpublishing.com

Copyright © 2025 **Ségu Séribandi**

All rights reserved.

Abibiman Publishing is registered under Hudics LLC in the
United States and in the United Kingdom

ISBN: 978-1-0685027-4-3

This is a work of fiction.

Cover design by Fred Martins

Printed at Clays UK

Author's Preface to the Rootless Nomad

What was then destroyed or ruined in Africa, and afterwards forgotten, proved hard to remember in later years.
— Basil Davidson, *The Lost Cities of Africa*

Among other things, The Rootless Nomad is about departure, displacement, the burden of recollection and the tortures of existence; it is an attempt to convey the prolonged tumults and agonies that ever so often assail inhabitants of all degenerate societies—and the nonconformists among them who by their temperament or circumstance become outcasts and situational survivalists who must grapple with a world so removed from familiar life. In confronting the ever-growing anticipation, and often inescapable suddenness of this change, the actions and choices of the characters in The Rootless Nomad (TRN) are held up to a mirror, which the reader might find indicative of our inclinations, psychic negotiations and self-justifying conclusions to animate or disrupt the logic of whatever we may perceive to be the goal of our existence.

In this vein, I have taken the liberty of naming the cities in TRN after the vanished or unremembered cities of Africa. By so doing, these cities and their names make no claims to represent the true scope and weight of historicity, for which this fictional work would be gravely insufficient, even though they may be said to be approximate in certain instances and, by this very fact, somehow keep the chords of remembrance alive. On the other hand, these cities in TRN also serve as vessels of parallelism to illuminate the roiling disconnection between what is known, however relative or slight, of the actual city-states, now lost to time and what our contemporary cities and states reveal about their joyless simulacra of those vanished epochs.

Perhaps, to situate TRN in its proper place, it is here preceded and succeeded by other stories whose leitmotifs and interpretations, though not wholly unrelated, will be left altogether to the reader's discretion. Only in this way can I faithfully declare, in time, that the reader was at full liberty to decide whether the stories are perceived in this or that light.

S. Séribandi
July, 2025

Departing Accra

Two weeks before Mensah left Accra for Harvard University, he had set about preparing himself feverishly for the inevitability of departure. His first order of business came under the uncluttering stage, which he set in motion by giving out the cheesy running shoes, washed-out jeans, and moldy banded shirts he had purchased several years ago from the flea market vendors at Circle. Next in order was the packing stage, which required leaping off, like a proper flyer, to Oxford Street, where he upgraded his clogs to Crocs and piled discounted sweaters, appliquéd with pheasants and bits of fanciful thingummies, on layers of full-length denim dungarees and radiant kente smocks. And there was no better time, he gathered, to seize his old man's terracotta portmanteau, sufficiently spacious and fashionable. The righteous man had no use for it anyhow. He was away in Central Malawi, fulfilling his presbyterial duties.

Harvard, the fabulous forge where he would be smithed and polished into a decent workpiece for the big people and their wandering albatross institutions, had finally become an unfolding reality after securing his American visa *the first time*. All those people with heads finer and circumstances lushier than his, yet rejected many times, some of them even now known at that ginormous American Embassy as perennial applicants, feeding an apparatus that is thrice determined to whittle them down until they no longer mattered, until their self-confidence was totally jiggered. This could only have been a divinely preordained escape; surely, God had sanctioned this journey right from his mother's womb, long before he knew the existence of Harvard in faraway America.

But he was so positively restless, he could not leave anything to chance. His uncle Kwabenya, the one who bankrolled the whole enterprise, had told him stories of how approved visas did not mean much until you got through the icy gate of Rhadamanthus, the one who guarded and held the exclusive power to grant or deny entree to the white man's world, the fabled home of the finest revolutions for human freedom.

"How difficult can it possibly be?" He had asked, naively, thinking his uncle an unrelenting exaggerator. After all, he argued, he had aced all his exams and aptitude tests, from WAEC and IELTS to SAT 1 and SAT 2, even almost did SAT 3 had he not protested to his uncle that he had written enough tests to prove he knew how to speak and write American English. All those exams, not in the slightest dissimilar from one to the other, just to convince them that he can be trusted, that he truly understood the one language he had been forced to learn since his birth. He would rather enroll on French lessons at Alliance Française or German lessons at the Goethe-Institut and go study at either of the two countries. Not that they were better, with all that Herero blood on the blighted souls of the Germans, and as for the French... better not to start. But in some ways they were different from America—Germany, in particular—no longer as conspicuous as America. So that's probably better.

"You won't understand, and I pray you never do," Kwabenya said, clucking.

"Eii, Bra, you say that too much. I hope you know am no longer a child," he returned, flying into a tirade in the next instant.

All this talk about what America wants and does not want: what about what he, Mensah, wants? Did nobody care that he, an embittered citizen of a conditioned third world country, wanted better for himself against all odds? He had trusted America all his life, defended and cuddled Americans in the face of all that propaganda, watched their movies, sang their songs, learned their language and atrocious slangs, and mastered the names of their celebrities, including the mediocre and the ones under the sod, hated their enemies in equal measure, ignored all those baseless, racist rumor about the savageness of life in Africa, those blasted canards about the blight that Africa was and wasn't on their righteous consciences. And he surely would have betrayed his mother despite all the love he had for her if America had asked. So why must America doubt and hate him so much that after going through all that trouble, he would be turned back right at the border? What else was needed that he had not done? At least, he had decided against England, he said, with all that noise about the far-right and their misguided determination to exact vengeance on immigrants, people they knew nothing about, branding them job-stealers, criminals, murderers, cannibals, and anything but white people's reflective underside, a self-reflection they believed was better dispatched and cast aside than legitimized, purified.

"Maybe you should just stay in Ghana..."

"Eii, Uncle K, you know that is not an option. What is the worth of a life here? 3,000 heads equivalent to one American? It was only by chance that it was confirmed by Sundaram. I want to matter."

It was nearly eight months before he was given a date to appear before the jurists at the consulate. Eight months, despite requesting an emergency appointment on the priority requests portal. He had secured the last bountiful scholarship he needed to cover his tuition, feeding, housing, and other such expenses four months before the beginning of the academic year that Fall. He would eventually defer his admission, with much understanding from the school and the International Students' department, to Spring. Still, it was something to be grateful for, the eight months. On YouTube, he had seen reports and commentaries about people waiting eighteen months, two years, some two and a half, and still getting rejected when they finally appeared before the consular officials—always the same unsmiling or oversmiling Obronis. The application process had tried every grain of patience in him, sucked half the life left in his solid frame, twisted his entrails, corkscrewing it stonily throughout the treacherous winding complexities of his online application, almost as if the whole shebang had been set up to dissuade him, to remind him of the limits of his dreams.

••••

"So now you won't touch me because you want to go to America?" Vanessa hurled her question in his face, her visage covered with petty sniggering, her voice struggling to choke back the incredulousness behind it.

"You won't understand," said Mensah before shrinking, quite instantly, at his sudden use of those same words he hated hearing from his uncle.

"See," he quickly recovered, "if everything goes well, you can have and devour me all you want. For now, you should be happy I even told you."

"Kwasia!" said Vanessa, scoffing at him as she shrugged, wondering how such an offbeat guy had even managed to bore a hole for himself in her heart. He was certainly in luck, this one.

All the same, she knew Mensah's enduring charm came not from luck but from his romantic quirkiness, his ability to effortlessly penetrate the clouded nebula that sometimes separated her from her immediate environment. She joined his secondary school at Kokomlemle at their senior level, and it was not difficult to notice Mensah: He was one of the two famous boys in their school. Mensah and Dozie, the Nigerian boy whom everyone loved to hate without reason, tease, and then celebrate whenever they returned from competing with those toffee-nosed sprigs of politicians at their over-priced blue-chip schools in East Legon and Cantonment. Whenever they returned with a gold-colored medal or trophy, which was often the case, the headmistress, Mrs. Bonsu, with her tortoise-rimmed glasses always sliding down her nose, would parade them on the assembly ground in a spectacle that sometimes went on for dozens of minutes with endless rounds of applause and shining teeth and orgiastic ululation. Short and muscly, Dozie's physique contrasted with Mensah's, who was almost as reedy as Stephen, the tallest and dullest boy in the whole of their set. But Mensah was bright, and he had a deep-black skin that glowed in the sunlight like the unique brilliance that jumped out of his mental circuitry.

Vanessa knew she found Mensah's special mind attractive, but also thought she liked him and Dozie equally, the popularity they shared and seemed to accept with easy pleasure, until both boys almost came to blows over who hugged her the most after school one warmish afternoon. Mensah, always the stoic and half-caring one, shrugged it off and stormed off to the school's library where he spent the better part of his after-school hours. Yet, when she told him she was feeling blue that weekend, he invited her over and read the complete *Our Sister Killjoy* to her for five unbroken hours. Here and there they nodded, hummed, giggled, laughed, and briefly googled German phrases and the curious word *Azania*. In his inmost parts, Mensah imagined what life must have been like in those days, when the book was written and became an African classic. When they got to page 75 and Mensah read two or so lines about lovers and their foolish acts, they turned to each other and shook their heads, their eyes wandering off into cavernous structures that only they, at that moment, could ever understand.

"Nice book," she said when Mensah finished reading, "but I don't get it. What is the message here?"

"Everything, don't you think?" he retorted.

"Hmm. You are exaggerating," she said, but in response, he rambled on, determined to help her see the depths of the words, which he himself did not fully plumb, and how the phrases leaped and burrowed into their heads in search of that Blackamoor spirit instinct with hobbled imprints of ancient civilizations buried in each and every offspring of the continent.

"Okay," he said, maybe he was exaggerating—but just a little bit; and never too much for the tenebrous void that even he knew they were yet to fill and may never fill up.

But that was over six years ago, and Vanessa had since re-read the book on her own at least three times since then, finding newly baked threads and masses of unriddled terms and expressions in it. As for Mensah, she thought nothing had really changed about him except his unflagging obsession with America and The Limeliters. Of course, he would deny it, insist he was not obsessed with America, nor Marty Robbins, Christina Perri, Bruce Springsteen, or that Harry Pollitt track, which always brought to his face the complete smile she thoroughly liked. A few times, she had chanced on him half-yelling, *Die Gedanken Sind Frei!* Yet his contempt for social life and tendency to interpret virtually everything in spiritual terms bothered her. His time at KNUST magnified all his subtle quirks alongside his innate brilliance, she was quite sure.

When she turned her back to continue *Perfect Match*, Mensah picked up his grey-colored laptop again and resumed his premental fisticuffs with reams of how-to videos on YouTube, watching one Indian content creator after the other ramble off their overlong tracts of forewarnings and dos and don'ts at an American student visa interview. His mind wandered off and back, wondering how he could possibly remember all these "simple" yet bewildering instructions. Yes, they all agreed there should be no lies, that America had horrifying eyes that rivaled God's ubiquitous character. But in the next breath, they also said he should only tell the truth where relevant, that he should only speak when there were questions to answer, and never answer such questions with more than one or two lines, lest he risked pissing off the jurist on the other side of the glass. Later that evening, when Vanessa was leaving for her mother's house, she told him not to fret and just be himself, and he thought she was right. But he was no longer sure what that meant, with all the lances of YouTube "expert" gimmicks pricking his cerebral matter.

The next day, when he woke up very early to his shrieking alarm, his languorous eyes fell randomly on one of his favorite quotes from Ayi Kwei Armah, sheltered in the laminated frame on his nightstand:

> Those who are blessed with the power
> And the soaring swiftness of the eagle
> And have flown before,
> Let them go.
> I will travel slowly,
> And I too will arrive.

He felt sufficiently roused and consoled by the words, and got up, ready to confront the behemoths at the consulate. At the bus stop, the gutter that ran beneath the passenger shelter discharged steams of horrid stench that galled his mind and made him feel that nearly everything was going to seed in Accra. The city was getting overcrowded, dirt and grime were replacing civilization everywhere, and now he had to wait longer than usual to get a tro-tro. The first one that stopped seemed eerily out of joint, and the only available space was a windowside seat on the last row, with all the sandwiched passengers shooting daggers at him and his vexing affectation when he refused to board. He could hear them calling him names as the driver drove off to his next stop but he did not give a tinker's cuss. By the time the next tro-tro arrived, he had only forty-seven minutes before his scheduled interview. Hesitantly, Mensah got in and sat close to the main door, hoping the residual spark Armah deposited in him that morning would not wear off. He sat with his legs clamped around his downward-poking forearm as the bus followed the usual course, with stops in various places that quietly needled him and left him on the verge of screaming Nananom, the spiritual vector for his long-gone ancestors. He would rather bring out his phone and exchange messages with Vanessa, but tro-tro passengers had no regard for anyone's privacy and would gouge out their eyes into his phone if they could.

By the time he got to the embassy, eight minutes before his eight o'clock interview, there was already a waiting line that stretched out into recursive outlines and intersected at different angles under the open sky, interconnected awnings, and shaded canopies like a sea of overextended squiggle. To his naked eyes, no adult age seemed missing in that file of America-bound supplicants; America, the land of deprived and starved Africans. All around him there were passport photographers, discreet document forgers, printing and photocopy experts, and drink hawkers, their voices and gestures hushed and loud as determined by the notions of the weather. A simple-looking lanky uniformed man assigned them numbers and gave him 80. *How* could this be? *Who* was in charge of this atrocity? Mensah thundered until someone came around to confirm the time of his appointment. When he confirmed that it was eight o'clock, they removed the zero in the initial number and asked him to move to the front of the line.

There, a pot-bellied Nigerian man came to check his documents, asked to confirm that the whole ball of wax was done to the taste of Uncle Sam, then asked him to leave his phone to someone before going inside. Started out of countenance, Mensah tapped his phone's screen and realized it was already past eight. *What a bummer,* he thought, the Indian guys on YouTube would surely have something to say about that. There was a squarish cubicle not far from the line, and he saw other supplicants handing their phones to properly armed soldiers, so he followed the short line and soon got the chance to turn over his gear. He feared there would be a price for that service, but they simply took his phone and keys, wrapped a stickum paper around everything, and made him write his name on it.

When he got back to the line, which was clearly not getting any shorter, the Nigerian man quickly beckoned him to advance. As he walked toward the next barricade of African gatekeepers, something about that giant embassy unsettled him, but he could not exactly place it. A door opened from inside, and then some brown-eyed uniformed fellow marched up and patted him down, first with his metallic hands, then with a batlike gadget that stayed green and noiseless throughout. Then they waved him to a long-legged gatekeeper with eyes like a hawk, and Mensah thought he was probably the most educated among them. The towering man took his time, lifted the double-colored hat that covered half his pan, scrutinized Mensah's passport and bounced his hawklike eyes from the document to Mensah's querying front, then nodded him on with half a smile when he was satisfied.

The turnstile rolled, and Mensah came up against another door, deep-tinted and doubtless heavy on the floor. The door did not yield when he pushed it, and then an officious voice started him with a "Stop!" The figure said nothing more to him, only knocked on the door twice before it opened up to another liveried figure who commanded access to the main compound. He was still letting out a long sigh when the unexpected stupefying light overturned his countenance. He was astonished by the enormous size of the property, the imperial dojo-like walls, at least twenty feet tall, and the limitless reach of the barbed wire spikes that crested the walls, extended in Olympian curls like an ancient city dreading the siege of barbarian Gauls.

Well, Mensah thought, he was right about America; with all the power and self-regard bursting within those walls.

"Forty-six," said a corpulent lady with nose rings who passed him a numbered piece of paper and gestured him toward the rows of empty plastic chairs under the silky tarpaulin cover, canopied by pooching neem trees and a concatenation of exquisite flowers that formed a circumference around them. The woman sitting close to Mensah, with a fat-cheeked baby on her legs cutting a caper, must have perfectly read his half-frazzled pan when she told him the line was moving quite fast. That they would soon be asked to come inside. Not long after, they were in the hall, which furcated narrowly into two halves, with a queue of manifold visa supplicants stretched out in a straight line on the sinistral side. On the right, a string of seven or so glass-covered enclosures delivered varying judgements to the supplicants. The first three cubicles were consular officials wearing the star-spangled lapel pin, and their task seemed to be to prepare the supplicants for the ruling of the Obronis who declared the actual verdict.

As the column advanced and Mensah edged closer to the frontline, a frosty sensation tingled the small of his back as he watched two of the Obroni cubicles, in particular, turn the supplicants' profiles from nervous smiles into abject let-downs. Instinctively, he launched a battery of mental calculations to predict which of the enclosures would be his lot, and how best he might gather himself now to avoid an unwanted outcome, desperately hoping misfortune would not be his portion. After all, he had avoided getting too close to Vanessa the week before, erected parapets against all intrusive thoughts and welcomed only positive ones, so now it was God's turn to reward him with visa favors.

Of the remaining cubicles, there was one on the farther end of the stretch from which supplicants emerged with holographic smiles, and there was the other one he just could not seem to figure out. The young man before Mensah was visibly jumpy, and Mensah recalled how the Indians had strongly warned against this. When it was the young man's turn to approach one of the menacing enclosures, he retarded his motion, feigning unawareness until the cubicle's Lycurgus, seeming out of humor, shouted "Next!" and everyone's attention suddenly turned on the lad, who now had no other option but to meet his adjudicator, bad or bad. Mensah wished he could comfort the young man with the words of Lamprius, the Soothsayer. But it was already his own turn now.

"Passport," the schoolmarmish jurist demanded.

Mensah handed it over, silent as advised by the Indians.

"Name?" asked the tight-faced inquirer on the other side of the glass.

"Mensah Kufuor."

Then she smiled, without reason, and Mensah wondered what he had done to cause that.

"Why do you want to visit the United States?" she asked, her eyes moving between the doobries on the escritoire and Mensah's serious countenance.

"To study at Harvard."

The slim lady looked up, her features bursting with the spirit of inquiry, and then she paused, seeming to wait for more...

"For my Master's. Mechanical Engineering," Mensah quickly added.

"Do you have your admission letter?"

"Yes," Mensah said as he passed on the document to her, alongside other documents, including a letter with the school's logo and official letterhead design, covering the details of scholarships awaiting him once he secured his visa.

One of the Indian creators had advised that he should add all relevant documents to any single document requested after his passport. They may not ask for more, the content-maker had said, and the applicant needed to be a "burra" supplicant, whatever the word meant, so that the official would be much more inclined to stamp their passport.

After going through all the documents, she slowly raised her head, adjusted her glasses with the tip of her index finger, almost aping *The Professor* in *Money Heist*, then asked, "Will you stay in the United States after your program?"

"I plan to return to Ghana to contribute my skills at the Ministry of Engineering." This was the question the Indian creators said never to answer with a yes or no, so he felt a sense of relief when he delivered the answer exactly as he had practiced. She then asked how soon he would like to travel.

"As soon as possible," he responded, almost going off about how he had deferred his admission once already and would rather be given his passport *immediately*. But thankfully, he held back his tongue. He had read somewhere that to speak and not to speak is a cultural art form among Africans, and the only reason Africans have survived as a people was due to their consciousness and mastery of this fact.

Soon after, the adjudicator raised her head from the escritoire and said he should keep refreshing his email, that his passport would be ready in a week. She did not dip her hand in the contrived receptacle glued to the artificial wall of her cubicle. He thought this was perhaps a good sign, as those he had seen receiving a copy of the sheets in that repository had left the hall with arid faces. Mensah thanked her, and as he trundled to the exit of the hall he was not sure whether to smile or dread what was to come after. The whole process had felt capitally mechanical, and something whispered to his mind that he had really been a "burra" supplicant.

When he finally got outside, reprising the whole gamut as he had done on his way inside, except that this time there was no shakedown, the wind touched his flesh in a way that announced the difference of the world outside. A rash of heat colonized his skin by degrees, and he felt ready to return home and start refreshing his email.

· · · ·

Three days later, Mensah was eating Banku and groundnut soup at a kiosk in the neighborhood when his doomscrolling on Instagram was suddenly disrupted by an email prompt.

Dear Applicant,

Your F-1 visa is approved.

Your passport is ready for collection at your chosen DHL location: DHL Teshie – GHS 250.

The passport number of document to be collected...

• • • •

He did not finish the email before ringing up his uncle.

"Bra, they approved it! They have approved my visa! They gave it to me!" he found himself screaming with a buzz, even though he had intended to keep his voice subdued as much as possible. The kiosk owner, the only one around at the time, was smiling broadly like a Smilodon, her wall-eyed sight radiating hesitance and delight while Mensah listened to his uncle offer his avuncular congratulations and thanks to God.

"Da Nyame ase[1]," he said.

Then Kwabenya told him he was in luck, that his been-to friend, Prince, who held an American green card was planning to return to Atlanta around the same time Mensah would be leaving Accra. He would try to put Mensah on the same flight with Prince. Mensah spent the following weeks preparing eagerly with the help of Vanessa. She would spend roughly half of those weeks at Mensah's parent's house, causing his mother to ask both of them what they planned on doing about each other after Mensah's departure.

"Ma, we will figure it out," Mensah had said, brusquely brushing the question aside like a fly in their ointment.

On the day of his departure, Prince's glossy-colored Mercedes Bus was at the Kufuor's to convey Mensah to the

---

1   We give thanks to God.

23

airport. Mensah's mother rode shotgun, chatting to the driver about her son's pilgrimage and the de novo experience ahead of him. Prince settled in the backseat, his crossed legs stretched out on the collapsed row of seats in front of him while he scrolled through his phone, nibbling a gingernut cookie. Vanessa and Mensah's hands were interlocked on the leathery seat as the latter looked through the tinted window of the bus to the street signs and telecoms banners advertising deals with no other intent than to overpromise and under-fulfill. In ritual fashion, Mensah hummed to Tracy Chapman's *Crossroads*, oozing from the piece of earbud tucked in his left ear. He felt himself reassuringly stirred, as he had been all week, by the evocative tune and repeated cadence.

But as they got closer to the Airport, Mensah felt a sinking feeling creeping up on him, and instantly he told himself he was going to get the better of it. What was it about this hollowness anyway? He had read stories of people recounting a wonky-headed flatness they felt whenever their lives were about to take a gloriously remarkable turn. He was determined to have a different experience, and so instead of indulging the sinking feeling, Mensah allowed himself to fantasize about the things he would do once he got to America: he would travel to Rosa's Cantina in Texas and sing El Paso to the phantoms of Marty Robbins until he was thoroughly fagged out. He would look for that genetically engineered prodigy in *Kyle XY* and those ladies who blissed out his life, or whose lives he blissed out. No matter, he would google their names later and also look up those pretty feisty gymnasts he fancied leading to the altar in *Make It or Break It*. Then he would go to Denzel Washington's next public appearance and tell him how he always thought of the legend whenever he had to say "My man!" He would post a snail mail to Viola Davis and tell her everything he could never forget from *The Woman King*, *Fences*, and *How to Get Away with Murder*! He would attend Lupe Fiasco's next show just to pit his wits against the brainiac, then he would go down to wherever to tell Nas how ravishing he always felt whenever he listened to his rap. Oh, what promise the future holds! So much to do in America!

At the Kotoka International Airport, Prince's favorite page helped them with their luggage as they left behind faces, feelings, memories, desires imagined and unfulfilled, and the misleading overtones of ease that invariably enveloped the city of Accra and wherever you found yourself in Ghana. Mensah turned one more time, and he waved to Vanessa with such affectionate impressions that one would be almost not surprised if he had gone back. When they disappeared into the ocean of pilgrims at the airport, Vanessa's phone blipped and she brought it out to see Dozie's notification that he was returning to Ghana soon. She smiled as she returned the phone into her jean pocket: One was on the horns of departure, so it made sense that the other had chosen to return.

The Rootless Nomad

PART 1

Everything, every human being could not be without its own Èsù in its constitution; it could not exist, nor could it be aware of its existence.

— Nicholaj De Mattos Frisvold
Ifá: A Forest of Mystery

1

It had been thirty-six months to the day since The Nomad fell into his lot, and though he did not set out to be one, he was merely a bust and listless nomad at this point.

The straitened scope of his life could no longer be gainsaid. His diaphanous paisley fabric shoddily fastened to nails on the mildewed window wall, in holes and pallid, reinforced an aura of deadness that swallowed his boxy foxhole. His mattress, which had visibly gone to seed, jostled for space with a rickety press which he used as storage for his evanescing cheap effects. A clutter of odds and sods fanned out unevenly and manifested clumsily, indeed deliberately, across the narrow interval which separated the window wall from the one close to the door—thickly cobwebbed at the gable and fractured at the perpendicular. The dishevelment of his foxhole and his evident lassitude had become a kind of implicit *de profundis* for intergalactic intervention.

'Not to worry,' The Nomad said to himself, his mouth funnelling out like the blooming of narcissus bulbs, 'I should like to think there are other nomads like me out there. Indeed, it is plausible that all humans are nomads; only some are more dignified than others.'

But he doubted this in the lucid corners of his mind. He was not in doubt that there were other nomads out there, 'but we all cannot possibly be nomads; there seems to be too many contradictions to disprove that,' he misdoubted.

Staring into the rafters above his head like a cryptic scratch-board stippling, he continued, 'It is, perhaps, more rational to think of nomadic creatures in two ways: a rooted nomad and a rootless nomad.' He paused and nodded as if he was beginning to penetrate a convoluted gossamer.

'If,' he continued, 'one were to think of nomadic life as a fleeting itinerant delectation, then one would classify artistic ensembles, missionaries, ghastly pastoralists, grey nomads and their likes, whose wanderlust and solipsistic jaunts render momentary birds of passage, as rooted nomads.' His eyes wiggled, then he nodded again, slowly, in a conscious attempt to not doubt himself as the words streamed through his gapehole.

'But,' he again continued, 'if one were to think of a perennial vagabond, whose memory of home has become distant and blurred, and whose basic understanding of human dignity or relative comfort has become muddled in misery due to the vagaries of unintended vagrancy, then the idea of a rootless nomad should be tangible. I am a rootless nomad.' He concluded, letting himself sink into a vacuum of existential mysteries at the same time.

A tall, wiry, innocent-looking bewhiskered man of retro taste and assertive mould; by obtainable standards, The Nomad was a man whose path indicated an upward rise back in his home country, Audoghast. His modest abode was situated in a placid cul-de-sac south of that patch, and he particularly took how it was peopled by a near-equitable proportion of the lunch-pail precariat and plebeians. That peculiarity seemed to have kept him in a neat loop of cognizance, in direct touch with uncorrupted reality. He enjoyed the comfort of his home and luxuriated in its lares and penates. Every now and again, he drove around in a homespun motorcar which he soulfully favoured for its simplicity, though he called on the mechanic about twice or so a month—not because the car was particularly problematic but because of his own finicality.

And whenever his apartment became fuggy, often because his neighbourhood suffered from a moribund power structure, he would saunter down to the grovy belt at the tip of the cul-de-sac on which his abode was situated, and sit close to a towering cask that was quite coniferous in length. The cask sat in the middle of a camphor tree, a guanacaste, and a few saplings that ringed it and disgorged collected water in spasmodic streams. But The Nomad viewed the cask in a way most people didn't: he attached a mystic bent to the fitful disgorgement, and was crestfallen whenever he was at the grove and the cask disgorged nothing, often for lack of rainwater. He was greatly chuffed by rainfall and frequented the grove during this pluvial period which lasted between the third to the seventh month of the year.

But the droughty days were bleak and difficult, and The Nomad was loath to go near the grove during this period, given his fear that a dry cask presaged an undesirable occurrence. He had essayed to dare the potency of this sinistrous premonition a few times while he was in Southern Audoghast, instinctively scoffing at anything that seemed to antagonize his self-adjudged apotropaic immunity. But, each time he did, his cheek was bruised as if the dry cask was in perfect unison with fortuity. And yet each instance belied the trails of happenstance, so that one dry quiet morning, he decided he would be unwise to underappreciate the foretokens of a dry cask.

••••

The Nomad had three friends: Ìgè, Ajégbèmí, and Lánléhìn. For a long while, he was loath to call them friends: he often felt a sting of contradiction whenever he strove to use that word, and he was all too perplexed about the unlacquered meaning of friendship and if it was at all in esse. He knew he could easily distinguish a foal from a fowl, but he couldn't say the same for a friend or those who professed the ideal just to stab one in the back. *The lines between friendship and its opposite are blurrier than the eyes can see*, he would often say to himself. All the same, it took him only a while to admit, that if all else was wanting in his existential journey, he could boast a smidgeon of friendship in those three.

Ìgè, rangy and agile, exuded the quality of a firm protector on matters in which his friends were concerned. He was thoroughly invested in how The Nomad decided on his unconcealed intentions, and though he was sometimes rash with his decisions, he had a penchant for seeking to rid The Nomad's sight of motes, especially the pestiferous ones.

He knew, for instance, which lot to avoid and which to seek out when The Nomad was about to purchase his first car. He knew the lot that replaced its finer car parts with mediocre ones and those who only sold lemons, always as swift as an arrow to reveal their game. He would often boast about his autodidactic knowledge of cars whenever he had the chance, although he worked as a cigar distributor in Southern Audoghast. It took a while to find something within the swell of The Nomad's pockets, but in time, they found a self-shifter of beefy composition and an impressive poke at a kosher lot choking with varieties.

Ìgè was also a dipsomaniac and hard drinker: he drank like one who had a canister in his gut, except it was in fact flat. There were days he would visit The Nomad's abode with two, sometimes three bottles of hard liquor and throw down the gauntlet for the drinks to be finished on the spot. He only attempted to backtrack his alcoholism after he suffered a spell of delirium tremens, during which he reluctantly forswore alcohol for two weeks at the hospital. Notwithstanding that deterrent spell, Ìgè could not shake off his craving for strong drinks any more than he was readily disposed to welcoming the full-fledged kryptonite in his system.

There were nights when Ìgè led the way in his and The Nomad's night-time cruising to happy hunting grounds, and they would both settle into their decadent indulgences without recourse to the reins, slugging, giggling, and frolicking in the ample possession of their pliant lady companions. Ìgè, however, was religiously industrious. He had no regard for shiftlessness and disdained men who were work-shy.

Lánléhìn was the even-tempered one. A college factotum by day and carouser by night, he had a dial that seemed plastered with a perdurable smile. His beer belly jutted out in a locked contest with his flaccid chest, and he was incurably fond of enormous women, those with derrières that wiggled and waggled without end. As a married man, however, he abhorred two-timing and brooked no scruples in professing where he stood straight from the shoulder. One Friday night at a seedy dive in town, renowned for its uniquely sapid black bullhead pepper-soup, about twenty minutes' drive from The Nomad's abode, Lánléhìn spilt his guts to The Nomad, Ajégbèmí and Ige—and up to a point his words pricked their flesh like pungent tines.

'If you three can be avidly loyal to your barbers, as I know you are, then—' he turned his goggling eyes towards Ìgè—'you, you can be loyal to your two wives. You have no reason to be with that scarlet woman you call girlfriend.'

Ìgè unbarred his mouth, gaped at Lánléhìn for a while and looked longingly to Ajégbèmí and The Nomad, as though he badly needed them to say something in his defence. But Lánléhìn had little time for his piddly sham, so he craned forward, fixed his mildly captious gaze on Ajégbèmí and The Nomad, and rolled his head as if their case was a bit direr.

'The two of you need to decide whether you want to be Oshaka or Oshoko—this or that; you simply should not be both,' he volleyed, playing his right hand as though he were coordinating moving traffic. Then, he relaxed his spine against his plastic chair, quaffed the chilled beer in his drinking glass, exhaled heartily, swung his thighs like a deflated tire, and evinced a self-approving smile.

Neither The Nomad nor Ajégbèmí was married, and both were something of a louche. Ajégbèmí remained stuck to his chair, a cultural historian and chain-smoker, pulling on and puffing his cigarillo with a quiet air as sidestream smoke branched out in updraught currents; but a queer smile soon creased his dial, as though the sign he needed to burst had arrived. Then, unhurriedly and steadily, he croaked his strangled throat, as if to rid it of phlegm, and began:

'You know, Lánléhìn, I find it hard to understand how you can chastise us with a straight face for the same thing which you are guilty of,' he said, stealing a sidelong glance at Ìgè and The Nomad.

'Or,' he continued, 'was it not this past Wednesday that we saw your… what does he call her again?—' looking to Ìgè for some help to fetch the words, but Ìgè shook his head doubtfully, and so did The Nomad—although they both looked approvingly, so he continued.

'No matter, I am sure you know of whom I speak; you are always bonking that nymph at least twice or so a week. Why, then, do you think your intrigue deserves approval and ours doesn't? Ehn, Lánléhìn? Or, is there some contorted idea behind your dalliance that we need to unearth?' he asked assertively, albeit peaceably, as he ran his meaty tongue across his sooty lips, slightly flicked his smoke and continued his wonted puff.

Lánléhìn grinned for the same reason he did when this matter was cursorily hinted at a couple of weeks before. But to all intents and purposes, he was quite pleased to put the matter to bed now.

'He who seeks clarity to a trodden path is bound to find answers,' Lánléhìn began, quite glacially.

'What you seek to understand is simply what we call consensual nonmonogamy; if you like, call it polyamory. You see, we have agreed to see other people outside our marriage, although they have to be approved by the both of us.' He paused, and passed his gaze on their obscure faces, as though intent to vicariously discern their pulse. Then, he continued.

'For me, I do not have to worry at all since I and my dear wife, Àárín, have a mutual interest in women only. As I always

37

say, we are both very happy in our marriage; and I'll rather polyamory than besmirch my vows to Àárín with perfidious entanglements. This way, we are both aware and make the decisions together.'

Suspecting an omitted detail, he swiftly added, 'since none of you has ever asked with any convincing curiosity—I thought to hold out on sharing until a day like this when there is some degree of interest…or, shall I say, a bogus charge!'

For a brief second, they were incredibly quiet, each trying to digest what he had just heard and working up his reaction. Then, almost in unison, Ajégbèmí and Ìgè stamped their tiddly feet and threw their arms in the air simultaneously, bursting in the chorus—'Baba Agbalagba!'

'Oh, you scoundrels!' he bantered.

Their guffaws rent the atmosphere and the other carousers almost felt the vibrations of their chests as they erupted in hoots of mock accolades.

Then they settled down to the eager lips of The Nomad, boggled and poised to stretch the matter a notch, as he began to unravel his thoughts:

'Seriously, though, Lánléhìn, don't you think this universal rave over polyamory is becoming too diffused in our world; that it is serving a sinister purpose of perhaps ensuring monogamist relationships are banished to the boneyard of anachronism?'

'Er… I understand you,' said Lánléhìn, his halting phiz vanishing soon after. 'But not quite. I think, it is an affirmative expressionistic act—you know, like the spreading of wings to flap about the boundless scope of the skies. At the very least, it keeps people honest and kindles their spiritual essence. And, I think, it emphasizes an unusual defiance of prosocial conditioning, weaving humanity together in a sensually phenomenal way that binds all to their monophyletic source. In a sense, it is a rather selfless efflorescence of the Franco-philiac ménage-à-trois—'

'Franco- what?' Ajégbèmí interjected gruffly as silence stiffened the air. 'Don't tell me you are unaware that many of our ancestors were polyamorists long before the coinage of that word? Even long before ménage-à-trois became a thing for the French? Listen, it was known as having 'companions' in Walata, and was the norm for both married men and women of that medieval civilization of this same continent that we call Great Sahara. But, let's not deceive ourselves here; this whole notion of sanctifying extramarital indulgences is purely a matter of hedonistic debauch. People just want to unmuzzle their carnality—'

'Tell them!' Ìgè piped up.

'If you pry deep,' Ajégbèmí continued, 'you would likely find that it is, for many polyamorists, an escapist way of upending a dysphoric reality. There is no emotional or spiritual hankering which is so drastic that only polyamory could positively gratify.' He concluded, whilst Ìgè nodded vigorously in agreement.

'The funny thing,' said The Nomad, 'is that Lánléhìn speaks of polyamory as though it were some canonized thing, some redemptive pietistic obligation. See, my friend, I do not think you are in any position to ethicize your polyamory whilst chastising us. I believe you would have done the same, if not worse, if you were shod in our shoes. If we don't remember anything, we remember your bachelorhood days, and you were just as ruttish as we are presently. See, I don't think you have been more faithful in your marriage than any of us would have been if we had the same constant gratification as you do. If, as we

39

speak, you find me a pliant belle that would revel in polyamory with me, especially if her tilt is towards bonking women only, just like your woman… my friend, Heaven forfend I would not declaim polyamory to the whole world.'

Almost simultaneously, the whole quad burst into heartful convulsions. Lánléhìn never sought to stretch the matter further. Besides, there were other non-issues to shoot the bull about.

．．．．

At this point, The Nomad could feel a pool of unsummoned blobs congregating on his brow, a branch streaming down his temple while another seemed to be rolling down his sunken cheeks. His eyes started briefly in their socket, as he swiftly essayed to remove the unsummoned congregants from his dial. Almost absentmindedly, he swabbed his bristled backhand across his sticky cast, raised his right leg chevron-like, towelled his backhand with his pagne loincloth, and repeated the gamut. He looked up to the white concave blades which formed a dome manqué above him and was struck by the fact that a fan had been whirling all along while he excreted perspiration. Quickly, he jumped to his feet and increased the fan's speed, and only then did he notice the swelling between his limbs. He tucked the jutting rod back in its sheathing, though it jutted out a few inches still. Then, he returned to his deep-set mattress, this time laying sidewise.

His intention was to cogitate on his miserable condition— to dissect the events which precipitated his nomadism and to think up ways to obviate his once-glistening life trajectory from utterly going down the pan. But no sooner had he willed—or so he thought—to make portraiture of those events than his mind was winched in a totally different direction. And all he could see was the poker-faced one, Ajégbémi.

Instantly, he recalled one of their Grape Lane promenades, as they knew them to be, in Southern Audoghast, and grinned lusciously. It should have ended there, but as he essayed to sheer away from that grain of distractive fancy, he was again winched in its direction so that, irresistibly, he began to relish how that crepuscular dalliance played itself out. This, he began to do without any prior intention to direct his thoughts thither. Ajégbémi, he recalled—jerking his pate upwards in fits of fleshly glee—in his characteristic eagle-eyed element, fully licentious and on the make, nodded apace towards someone they were driving towards in the middle of their chatter, and immediately jogged The Nomad's attention, swaddled in what seemed a bit of mad-headedness. It was a zaftig member of the oldest profession that he could not resist, and as it turned out neither could The Nomad after slamming on the anchors at a guarded distance.

'Caution,' The Nomad warned, relating how his last experience on the same turf had tainted his Grape Lane palate. He had driven home that pleasant-seeming night, brimming with expectation while hoping his Grape Lane catch would nicely pass as another notch on his bedpost. But then, he found himself repeatedly yelling *Caramba!* in his mind each time he learned something new about her that gave him the pip. As they inched farther into the night, exchanging glances and chewing the fat, he would realize she had padded her breasts and backside, and that her bare form was scantily patched with blemished underthings, leaving him no choice but to ask her age, which was how he learned she was sixteen. *Sixteen!* He was still contemplating the moral atrocity when, all of a sudden, she asked for something to eat. Then he committed the error of offering her a glass of water and a loaf of bread, at which point she clumsily soddened each broken chunk and solidified his disgust. Hurriedly, he scratched her palm and sent her off into the night.

And now, though he preached caution, it was merely a desultory one: He had agreed to this unplanned promenade, albeit reluctantly, silently hoping to find a relishable grape and, deep in his mind, he could not wait for Ajégbèmí to fetch this particular one, which the latter did at warp speed. Then, donning a feigned disinterest, The Nomad muttered pleasantries to Binta—for that was her name, or eke-name—belying Ajégbémi's raunchy extolments of the *grande horizontale*.

'Is it real?' The Nomad was quick to ask, referring to the plumpness moulded on her backside. 'You can touch it if you want,' she said, turning around while she coated her face with suggestive features. Both The Nomad and his confederate had a contrived sobriquet for grape-hunting, and each shared his with Binta—Ajégbèmí as John; The Nomad, Samson. But Binta's coal-black skin and fluty voice soon dissolved The Nomad's dissimulation.

And, presently, as The Nomad sunk deeper into the vortex of his satyric reminiscence, he felt a deluge of delightful warmth, recounting to the touch every detail of that night's troilism: the lust-ridden grip of Binta's flirtations, her lustrous eyes, velvety skin, bewitching slithery striptease, her bosomy fondling of his manly bits, the thrilling sensation of her mobile rounded coverage, the rhythm of it, the overpowering intensity of her fellatio, the splendidly controlled rhythm of it, the double lancing and thrusting by himself and Ajégbémi, Binta's torrential discharge, and the final act of his own manliness, his vigorous onanistic emission, splattered over the corpulent form of Binta. He remembered them all.

Like a streak of lightning, the sudden rush of these memories plunged The Nomad into a dark flush, and in what seemed a meld of fading pleasure and palpable desolation, his heart palpitated in cadenced frustration, and in his head welled up convulsions of unfathomable eruptions. At that moment, he began to feel his head distend like it was going to burst; his veins jutted out of his skin like a caravan of furious streams, his eyes bulged ominously like a wild-eyed beast, tranced in his own vulnerability and his helplessness to end it—feeling, as it were, as though he was being shuffled away by a mystic, relentless eddy. Oblivious of his convulsive descent, though also aware of his sagging equipoise, he got up on his feet and began to sprauchle back and forth—yet his head remained glommed on to the tattered headboard.

'How did I get here?' he queried, toing and froing with trudges that seemed to suggest his legs becoming heavier with every teeter.

'How foolish I must be to exchange comfort for hardship. For how long will my life continue in this pitiable state? I have wallowed in my lonesomeness for so long I am now jaded by this very state which used to bring me comfort.' He lamented, as his mind continued to scurry about in different directions.

Now inclined, he felt like his eyes were shut and wide-opened at the same time. Suddenly, they fell on the crater and it seemed like a limnic eruption which was inexorably determined to slug him.

'This is a trap,' he thought, feeling lost, boggled and in the saddle all at once. He stood there for what seemed an eternity, still fixated on the crater, but now with an admixture of misdoubt and surrealism.

'What if I fall in and start chasing a white rabbit? Who will look for me if I find myself in Pluto's Lower World or Tutuola's bottomless abyss?' his mind mumbled suchlike questions, and he would sometimes bob his head as if he was in absolute harmony with his thoughts, as if he was even thinking at all.

The crater again seemed to be inviting him to take a dive, daring him to plunge into its arrant darkness—a void so magnificent he abruptly felt he could create a new world with a few spoken words. His arms, folded for a while in an interlocked posture, remained suspended at chest length and interacted in hushed tones. He took a pause, grinned and suddenly the crater disappeared and all he could see next was the hollow in his mattress. He tried to sink himself into the gape but all that ensued was unrelieved stasis—he had moved but only remained hitched to the same spot. At once he felt blanketed by an extremely bright nimbus, and currents of flitting breeze descended on the curly-wurly mop forming a parasol over his head. He couldn't baulk the force of the air from sinking into his pate as rivulets darted through his spine and his skin horripilated to the gliding soothing waves.

Only then did he realize he had been sitting all along, and his slippage through the crater, the Lower World and so on had been a volant spin in a world of phantasm, which his mind conjured up whilst he was trapped in a psychoactive seine. At once, he remembered he had pulled on the Johnson-supplied tea by his bedside before laying sidewise; and then he giggled and laughed at himself for no reason.

But all of a sudden, he felt pathetic, shattered and lost. He felt the wind of vacuity romancing his bone-weary soul and could not help but mourn his own lonesomeness. He had no idea that smidges of water had begun to rim his eyes and soon, trickled down his sunken cheeks and moistened his dry lips. Then, he began to greet. Profusely. He felt the sting of the brackish seam on his lips, and his tongue became tangy. He suddenly got up and shuffled himself to the door, only to again drag himself back to the deep-set mattress like the deuce, and plonked into its recess, as though he was not in control of his marbles.

Audoghast is a place of great history. Aeons ago, it overflowed with effervescent inhabitants and was distinct for its cultural, social, and economic puissance. It had kings who knew what role they held within the realm that shielded them and their rich and diverse populace. Indeed, palisades and shelters of colourful hues ornamented the landscape, and humans with diverse interests delighted in their unhurried and satisfactory wanderings on that spirited patch. This ci-devant Audoghast abounded in all kinds of treasured articles and artefacts, even superabundant scholarship and literature now plundered, paraded by humans of diverse shades and purposes. In those days humans and flora and fauna had a distinct prestige verging on the Golden Age.

When The Nomad was still immature, his grandmother, Mama Jebba, would sit under the benign penumbra of moonlight with him and others—young and old—in his hometown of Abiri in Southern Audoghast, once the seedbed of finely crafted terracotta heads now lost to time. Mama Jebba would tell stories of great dynasties and empires, which flourished in the Great Sahara before they were desecrated by the unlooked-for expedition of proselytizers and their crusaders-at-arms, who spoke as ghoulish emissaries of Supreme Beings—one dominating the Arabian patch of the Earth and the other, supposedly omniscient and all-powerful, the demiurge whose caritas—championed by the Holy Saintdom from Albion—was said to animate and commute the depravities of all existence, including the people of Audoghast who had their own cosmology, theology, theogony, and even ideologies.

Mama Jebba would sometimes tell stories of gilded brindled canines and other furry critters in palatial estates in that ci-devant Audoghast, and how they were fed until their dewlaps drooped in glut and merriness. Their flabbiness made them sui generis and they were always laired up with the bountiful gold of the land. These ancient canines ate from golden plates, slept on golden mats, and sported custom-made gold pendants, bearing names of primordial city-states and especial kings who were believed to be a breed apart for their sagacity. Yet, Mama Jebba sometimes spoke of this ci-devant Audoghast in tragedian tones, for if there ever were a belle époque in that part of the world, the Audoghast epoch would stand out as one. She always ended by saying 'o ba ni, ko baje,' often translated by her into that famous Shakespearean apophthegm: 'all is well that ends well.'

—'But the Audoghast in which I was bred was not only different, it was a brutal place,' The Nomad bleated as he tried to extract his body from the recess into which he had plonked it a few hours ago. He had been half-awake for some minutes since his brief slumber ended and he was thrust into the discordant wail of the fan above his head, although his head seemed lighter at that moment and his thoughts seemed to be becoming coherent. His mind hearkened back to that distant past of which Mama Jebba often spoke, in which he wished he had lived and died as an avatar of spirited distinction for the bards of yore.

His lower spine ached as he struggled to lift himself. Seated, he tried to lean forwards and recline backwards and draw out himself at full stretch; but his muscles wouldn't yield to the hopeless callisthenics bend. He then tried to leap from his sedentary position but, at that instant, he felt assailed by a putrid foetor, as if he had been transposed to a charnel ground mouldering in decomposing cadavers, or dragged into a maze of rancid catacombs. He waved his head frantically as if to block out the wretched stench but the more he tried, the more intense the noisomeness. Then, all at once, he cocked his head sinistrally and was so disgusted he nearly took the air with fury. The culprit was the dumpsite which was only a stone's throw from The Nomad's foxhole, and he knew the twilight wind must have bumped the door a little inward. Gradually, he shuffled himself out of his deep-set entanglement and stumbled towards the sludgy door, slammed it with unsuppressed spleen, and stumbled back towards his mattress.

'You frigging pest!' he mumbled in his mind.

But no sooner had he begun to stretch his arms to precede his next descent into the recess than a grating creak travelled into his eardrums—from the dextral wing, and this time it was a different culprit. It was the pole-to-pole effect, as he named it, of the washroom door whose creaky response was a swift and constant attendant of all pettish attempts to open or shut the entrance door. The Nomad knew he was to blame for slamming the easily offended door in that manner, for the other door had no desire to resist the signal of the one to fling itself ajar.

He trudged towards the door, cautiously bent its knob, and closed it in a phlegmatic fashion: this was one of the several problems of the hovel in which he lived. The conduits that conveyed grey water and sewage from his decrepit washroom to the septic tank had been markedly clogged since the day he moved in, and he had repeatedly lodged complaints to the frumpy harridan who was his landlady, but she would always respond: 'boy, don't kill me before my time!'

You already have one foot in the grave, so why be a grump over the inevitable? he would fleer at her in his mind.

And there were times when she would take a walk down her more termagant path, swearing like a trooper. Too many things to complain about, too many things, but The Nomad had abandoned hope on such moony ideas.

He felt, perhaps too intensely, that his options were limited; that he had somehow ploughed into *nostalgie de la boue* without intently wishing it on himself. His foxhole at that point happened to be his sixth since he left Southern Audoghast, each lodging witnessing and solidifying his financial, material, and psychogeographic devolution. Hence, as far as that hovel was concerned, he had resigned himself to the reality that he was, willy-nilly, ensnared in a neither-nor actuality, a straitjacketed state of existence in which he had to struggle with unrelieved wretchedness.

• • • •

There was enough to fascinate one about the natural landscape of modern Audoghast. It distinguished itself as a striking paradox of nature: to the north were the barren plains and wastelands, mottled with dingy homesteads, a sparse but rich admixture

49

of intervening plateaux and a searing but tolerable climate. The south, on the other hand, unfurled itself in ensouled manifestations of urban sprawl and architectural *aggiornamento*: vivid edifices, galloping gentrification and fleshpots of capitalism, intermingled with rock-ribbed hills, virid woodlands, valleys, rolling downs, as well as coastal zones. And whilst Northern Audoghast was the natural habitat of breeders and traders of livestock, the yawning plateaux were home to farmers and textile weavers of all hues. The south, by contrast, had a distinct reputation for its depthless mineral reserves of petroleum, coal, iron, tin, copper, etcetera, trading farm produce and quintessential handicraft, predominantly pottery and sculpture.

There had been periods of unquiet calm and more periods of great turbulence in Audoghast, the most of which derived from nuances of interethnic incompatibilities and endogenous injustices. Northern Audoghast, on the one hand, was known to be mulishly yoked to Islam and the truculent tribalistic feudalism of the Fulbe. But Southern Audoghast, on the other hand— though tremendously yoked to Christianity than to Islam, and, in the main, only infinitesimally congenial to traditional religions— was essentially non-belligerent and relatively broad-minded.

One breezy night with Mama Jebba, about a week after one of his juvenescent birthdays which his mother had celebrated for him in style, The Nomad gave vent to a series of unresolved questions which his puerile mind was unable to puzzle out on its own.

'Mama Jebba,' he said.

'Ehn, Olowo ori mi?[2]'

---

2   A term of endearment.

'Why do you like to say that I bolt my food as if Northern cattlemen were chasing me?'

In response, Mama Jebba donned her characteristic mystique grin and retied her wrapper, which seemed to be giving to the volant breeze.

'Olowo ori mi,' she began, 'there are things that are beyond your grasp now, but since curiosity begets illumination, I have no doubts that there should come a time when some of the things I tell you tonight would become perfectly lucid to your mind.'

'Even if I don't understand, Mama Jebba, I assure you your words will not leave my retentive mind.' The Nomad said assuredly. He was rather old beyond his years, even in his juvenescence.

'I hear you, my son. You have asked an important question, and I would like you to listen to my answer regardfully. I am an old woman now, and someday soon, I shall be feasting with our ancestors…' she briefly hawked and spat out phlegm, smacked her lips, and then continued.

'A long, long time ago, when the father of your father's father, and the mother of your mother's mother, who was my own mother, were young and jolly, the fanatic descendants of King Hume of the Sefuwa Dynasty invaded our land at the tip of Northern Audoghast, killed many of our people, and even burned some alive. It was a truly horrible massacre.' She paused as if to gauge The Nomad's composure or disquiet, but his countenance was innocently vacuous.

'You see, the reason they attacked,' she continued, 'was because they wanted our people to know that they would all perish as kaffirs if they refused to convert to the religion of Islam. Now, you see, a great man known as King Hume had converted to Islam some eight hundred years or so before the attack, and the Kings and Potentates after him had sustained that paradigm as Mohammedans, usually for reasons that were purely economic and, sometimes, political. But those who attacked our villages when my mother and your great grandfather were alive believed that King Hume was wrong to have permitted animists and devotees of traditional religions to live peacefully without forcibly converting them to Islam or enslaving them during his reign. As fanatics, they believed in fundamentalist militancy, like some people called the Almohads and the Almoravids.

'Back then, as my mother narrated to me, the sectarians invaded our villages both day and night, and our people created groups of vigilantes to keep watch and defend themselves. But sometimes the sectarians attacked when people were either eating breakfast, lunch or dinner, and the majority had to bolt their food before they were called on to fight. As a result, that act of eating speedily before fighting the aggressive invaders became the origin of the saying which you have just asked me about. The saying might initially seem humorous, but I hope you can see that it is quite not?'

'Yes, Mama Jebba. I am shocked to learn that such an evil thing happened here in the past,' he said, quite assuredly, like one who truly dug the matter, though inwardly he was somewhat puzzled. Yet, at that moment, the grim anecdote settled as shards in his subliminal crevices, so that it might again be disinterred whenever the occasion summoned it.

'How did great-grandpa feel during this period?' he volleyed suddenly.

'From what I know, the poor man was distraught. And who wouldn't be? He was almost crushed by the burden of starting all over again, compelled to migrate to the south after he survived the last invasion by the skin of his teeth. He was truly devasted by the loss of friends and relatives to the crazed zealotry, perhaps even haunted by their spectral types because, for a long time, he remained disoriented.'

'But why were those fundamentalists never put to rout?'

Mama Jebba heaved a quaint sigh and played her hand in a cryptic manner as if she was at that moment too spent to dwell further on the matter. And that was how the conversation ended.

The Nomad knew when not to pester his grandmother. So he chewed his guileless questions and preserved them in his thoughts.

• • • •

In his claggy hovel some 2,000 kilometres from Audoghast, the thoughts of his juvenile exchanges with his grandmother, and her benignant indulgences, even didactic cultivation of his mind— which struck him now as similar to that of a dutiful Campesino, convinced of the fructification of her creative labour, regardless of her hostile milieu—sobered him as he made for the slough of soul-piercing reminiscences.

'How could I not have seen it?' he asked himself, recalling the pitfalls that marred his struggle for a better Audoghast where human dignity would supplant the monotony of platitudinal affirmations.

'Was it me? Or was it something or someone else? A preemptive strike, perhaps? Could there have been no other way—perchance a more decisive knobkierie to clobber the system into Hades?'

Inch by inch, he began to unfurl the events in his turbulent mind, one after the other, to re-examine the pitfalls and… 'well, for now, just re-examine the blasted pitfalls!' he suddenly lashed out at himself. Inwardly, he felt like he was being torn apart by myriads of poleaxes: he knew he had neither set out as a revolutionist to instigate the 'science of destruction,' in keeping with Nechayev's catechismal rubric, nor exhibited the radical iconoclastic spirit of Huey Newton. And this realization, that he had been non-radical and yet made to suffer, galled his psyche and at the same time baffled him to the hilt.

'When Hassan told me to either consent to his bidding or stew in my own juice of nonconformism, should I have pliantly acceded to it? Should I have seen the pointlessness of it all?' he queried.

'But that's only a blinkered construal of the case,' he continued, 'for I must not discountenance those who, like me, have suffered unquantifiable losses, and even those who breathed their last on that fateful day for our shared affirmation which was perhaps ill-fated from the start—'

Hardly that, he retorted in his querying mind.

Suddenly, he wriggled briskly from side to side as though he had stumbled on the nexus of the matter; 'could it have been… my conscience?'

'It must be! My better feelings, no doubt, continue to be my biggest impediment to being a full-blooded solipsist. For, if I had surrendered to fatalism and complied with Hassan's bidding, rejecting all self-sacrificing beliefs for accidie, stifling all rebellious instincts to the glory of inutility, refusing to yield to the pangs of my better feelings, which I truly gave a free rein of expression—perhaps an excess free rein it was—my back would hardly ache from the cruel torture of this unseemly mattress; neither would my nose be assailed by the stench of that fetid dumpsite and washroom, nor my ears lose all pleasure of luxuriating behind pacific doors.'

Nonetheless, The Nomad was at the brink of being totalled by the deleterious conditions of undesired nomadism, a dead weight so oppressive he had begun to regard himself as a cockchafer to the living, to all things, even the air he breathed that wouldn't stop being his.

Yet he felt something dynamic, a tinge of something which seemed to him supreme; something which seemed reserved only for people like him, for people whose sense of living derives from knowing that gnomic epistemic of Goldsmith, which at once he remembered; that the heart which is buried in a dungeon is no more precious than that seated on a throne. He, too, felt a grain of that epistemic light, and it seemed to warm the cockles of his heart, so that he began to feel himself being gradually retrieved from his despairing cavern.

But even that grain of light failed to alert him to his diaphoretic state, which had sufficiently caused his gauze loincloth to be soaked, in the same way the brackish sweat that pooled in his spinal concave plastered his sunken mattress, while tiny drops dribbled down his forehead. The electrical power was out, and a ghostly silence had engulfed his hovel.

—'Ogbeni! Ogbeni!'

The voice started him back to his airless surrounds, now fully alert that the sound he seemed to have heard from a distance was rather closer than earlier imagined. It was the boorish voice of Johnson, which sounded, as always, like the lowing of a cow. He quickly rived his hitherto catatonic spine from the sunken mattress, slightly stung by the resulting soreness, and shambled towards the door.

—'Ogbeni!'

The unmistakable voice and the mesomorphic type irrupted light-heartedly through his unbolted door, but at once startled by the impregnable darkness which enveloped The Nomad's hovel, and seemed to grope for a beam of light before calling out once more: 'Ogbeni!'—for that was The Nomad's *nom de guerre* in Niani. He told himself this was a necessary shield for an impermanent state, and if he ever were to go down under those circumstances, all the better!.

The darkness was in no time pierced by a penlight in Johnson's hand.

'Oh, here you are!'

For some reason unknown to The Nomad, Johnson seemed gaily, judging by his histrionics within the shades of The Nomad's hovel, which eventually culminated in what seemed to The Nomad a chain of arch questions.

'Are you all right? Have you been sleeping? What are you doing?'

'No, you tell me: what are you doing here?' The Nomad retorted, like one whose steadiness had suffered unsought disruption. He was nettled by the stridency of Johnson's voice, a habit for which he had issued several admonitions. But in his heart, he felt some relief to see Johnson who, he was quite sure, had come around to get him out of his hencoop, often towards some beneficial end.

Johnson, the landlady's only child and an unwaged physicist at the National Institute of Scientific Discoveries in Lower Kangaba, barely two years older than The Nomad, exuded an uncanny lenity towards The Nomad which belied the character of his mostly shrewish, hoary mother. How come Johnson had taken to him so, The Nomad can neither explain nor care to remember now. But surely, every dab of tea shared between them had brought them closer. It is known, also, that at the instance of Johnson, several nights had witnessed both of them partaking in the offerings of whatever tawdry watering hole would have them in Lower Kangaba.

'Well,' Johnson began, 'I thought you would like to go for a walk, I am feeling really peppy tonight and can use your good company.'

'You don't have to say it; that's rather obvious. But I don't feel like going for a walk. What, by the way, is the reason for your peppiness?'

'Hahaha. You are always not feeling like going for a walk. Do you somehow enjoy this reclusive existence? Is this how you wish to die; alone and dolorous?'

The Nomad looked expressionless and bleary-eyed, as though Johnson's words were rills on a shallow ground.

'Any road, I guess I have no other choice but to tell you now. You see, yesterday I was not feeling too well and felt like I needed to relax. But I didn't know whether to go to bed early and—'

'Johnson,' The Nomad interjected brusquely, 'if this is going to be one of your long-winded blatherings, I will suggest you put a sock in it, now.'

'No, no, no, just calm down. This won't take long at all. We don't even have time to waste as such. I promise. Any road, as I was saying, I didn't know whether to go to sleep immediately yesterday evening or stay up until later, to avoid waking up in the middle of the night. You know, whenever I wake up unintended in the middle of the night, I am disregarded by sleep until dawn; and ach, how it makes me cantankerous! But, this time, I decided to hit the hay when my fuzzy feeling started getting intense. Now, if I had known, I would likely have gone to bed earlier. Any road—'

The Nomad heaved a frazzled sigh and waved his head lamentably.

'Okay, okay,' Johnson said, suspecting he was beginning to push The Nomad's buttons.

'What happened was that I had a dream. It was very strange; you won't believe it. I was being chased by what looked like a straw-coloured bulldozer and kept running for my life. But something kept telling me to look back as if there was something else chasing me apart from the bulldozer. Any road, I finally decided to look back and guess what I saw?'

'A pillar of salt?' The Nomad returned.

'Come on, man! It was Digits. I saw scattered and lumped digits.'

'As in numerals?'

'Yes!'

'Okay, and?'

'Ah, yes! You know I sometimes visit the booth down the street, just to keep the body and soul together?'

'What booth?'

'Destiny of Man. The one after Tochi's shack.'

The Nomad paused a while, then responded gruffly:

'Well, you may as well go ahead!'

'Okay, okay. So, Destiny of Man is the lotto booth after Tochi's restaurant. And, well, the digits I saw were lottery numerals. I knew it the moment I woke up and could still remember them in real life. Normally, I forget my dreams completely, but not this time.'

'Good for you.'

'For me and you, Ogbeni! For me and you!'

Johnson's glee was now palpable to the touch, as he leapt in one jump to The Nomad's side, and hunched over as if to whisper a rumour for their ears alone—to be so discreet that even the mattress would not hear it.

'I won...' he said, 'I won *big*, Ogbeni!'

'Oh. Okay. That's good... for you.'

'What is wrong with you? Can't you see this is a good reason to be happy?'

'Yes. For you to be happy. But how it concerns me is still a mystery.'

'You know, you are just too stern sometimes. If I didn't know better, I would have said you were being a sulky washout.' Johnson said, as his profile betrayed crinkles of deliberate meanness and a touch of petty satisfaction.

'Well, on that you and I may agree with ease. Only washouts like me writhe in unrelieved gloom from darkness till the light of day.'

'Well, Ogbeni, I seriously couldn't agree less with you on that. Hear me, what you are going through now is merely a passing phase, a peculiar thermodynamic experience that is contingent on the degree of anthropic disorder in our world. We scientists call it the second law of thermodynamics. But, in general, what it means—and I know this is probably not what you wish to hear—is that things will eventually organize themselves in your favour, so long as you keep your mind open and keep your body and soul together, like me.'

'Mmm-mm, I see,' The Nomad murmured, staring vacantly at Johnson the same way he did when he was saying something in the past about black holes and mass and event horizon.

'Any road,' continued Johnson, 'that is really why I am here. We need to have some fun tonight. The money here with me should aid us in doing that—so long as we keep it simple and make no fuss.'

Hearing this, The Nomad at once felt a minuscule current of lustiness fizz through his veins. But his conceit lacquered it just well, hidden behind that veil of deceptive fogginess.

'First, I am too hungry right now to think of any joint,' was The Nomad's response, before he again continued. 'Your disturbance has plunged me into that biological blowhole of threshing hunger, which I would rather have avoided today. So what I am thinking now is how I would get something to eat, not to visit a joint to get wasted. Second, you, not me, are the one who needs to make no fuss; whether at a joint, or here in my room.'

'Food? Look at this man. You see, if we must, we will eat till our bellies bust before heading to the joint. That one is for sure. In fact…' he stretched out his curved leg, tilted a little to the left, fumbled about his right pocket and brought out some folded matter, which turned out to be quite a knot in his hand, fairly substantial than a pittance:

'Take this, you need to manage it for now,' he said, squeezing the wad into The Nomad's palm.

'Ach, my good man, thank you. This should keep me afloat for some time,' The Nomad said, feeling slightly abashed.

'See, Ogbeni, you are a good guy. I believe you will find your feet soon enough. Until then, we must stay alive and enjoy life as much as we can. So, get up and let's go have some fun.'

As he essayed to extricate himself from his recess, the partly soaked gauze scarf that passed as his loincloth began to unfasten, so he called both hands to the rescue quickly.

'Is that my mother's scarf?' Johnson asked, gaping at The Nomad's crotch, his voice invested with certitude.

'Yes, please don't tell her. The last thing I need now is to be ragged by your mother. I had to wash my underwear and shirt earlier, and this is all I could get outside to cover myself in the meanwhile.'

'That's alright, Ogbeni. You don't have to ask me that. But be sure to dust it well later, eh, I don't want my old trout visiting the doctor on that account...' Johnson quipped, as his cheeks formed into teeny smacks of tease.

• • • •

It was eighteen months ago—three months and a week before he moved into his current Niani foxhole—that The Nomad decided to sell off most of the clothes and prized shoes in his possession. When it came to shoes, he would often declare to his friends in Audoghast that he was one of the universe's 'victims of acquired tastes.' But his abject privation as a nomad had become so harrowing that he was on his beam ends and could not but sublimate his vain fondness into a meagrely rewarding enterprise. It was an expedient course which, after a long walk one day in the charring sun, a pushcart peddler in one of the rowdy flea markets satisfied quite generously.

••••

The Nomad had suddenly found some foison to move about briskly. He knew Johnson's appearance from the start was a benison shorn of guise. Now his long legs capered to cheery rhythms on their own, and his flat shoulders jutted out moderately, alive and in sync with the rest of his body. Briefly, he swivelled in the same spot, seeming to think of something for a while, then grabbed his schmatte towel which only covered half of his spare waist and made for the fence outside to which the clothesline for the ungated house was attached. He felt his pants and skivvy to see if they were dry and found both to be fit for purpose.

Freshened up and in motion, The Nomad was once again reminded, by the sheer horridness of life in his cruddy surrounds, that he was a sojourner in the dreggy part of Kangaba. In Niani, people were cast in funereal mould, each had a mire of their own, infants were condemned to worser fate than untended farrows, and the majority bustled about like fire ants on the trot, chasing shadows and languishing in penurious sludge. Despite nature's superabundance, Niani seemed the waste water of both Lower and Upper Kangaba.

The layout of the unmade road on which The Nomad advanced featured monotonous articulation of battered stalls, engaged vendors, unfuzzy patronizers, inscrutable pedestrians and other interwoven renditions of typical life in Lower Kangaba. There along his path, he was abruptly jolted by a sight he had yet to witness since his first day in Kangaba. The marching herd straggled along slowly in the same way they did in Audoghast, unworried by the rapid descent of dusk as passers-by walked by without alarm. In their trail were hardly any clods of cowpat. At that moment, The Nomad's mind hearkened back to his formative years in Audoghast, when he was often puzzled by what his embryonic mind perceived as a macédoine of peoples so different and disagreeable yet seemingly trapped in a consociational tinderbox. Those days when he was ireful whenever he walked through a road in Southern Audoghast bedaubed with cow dung or saw a stick-wielding herder, crouched down on his haunches to pass water at inappropriate public spaces in broad daylight. How he would screech dreadfully in his mind, shooting daggers in the direction of this or that capricious fellow caught in the act. Then he recalled the days he felt sorry for the hapless roadside traders, whose vending stalls were erected on the planked culverts which these heedless swine often made their targets and so arrogantly defiled. Even then, young as he was, he had concluded that these herders must take pleasure in being a pain in the neck of others, for how else to explain the haughty nonchalance, the absence of regard for spaces owned or treasured by the other residents of Audoghast? But now he observed in the herders of Kangaba a kind of orderliness he could not recall witnessing in his motherland, as though unwilling to reawaken those childhood sentiments he once had. Perhaps it was the way the herders of Kangaba acquitted themselves, their punky unthreatening gaits, easy smiles, even their fat scabless cows.

As they moved past one structure after another, Johnson's mind drenched in sober and quixotic ideas, The Nomad's eyes suddenly fell on the street hooligans in one of their predatory underbellies, 'and to imagine,' he said to himself almost instantly, 'that I used to think the hardest thing in life was to exist and do nothing,' shaking his head as though he were grieving his social conscience; and though that may be somewhat true, he was, in fact, more appalled by the nerve-wracking disaster which that underworld of hooliganism and intemperate sloth foretold.

'Why has doomsday not come?

Why does not the Last Trumpet Sound?

Who holds the reins of the Final Catastrophe?'

—queried The Nomad, as he remembered Ghalib.

'The irony of all this,' he mused as he galumphed next to Johnson, 'is that these young, shiftless yobs who diddle around day and night, may eventually be the Mercury to save this place from its Argus-surveilled destruction. For it seems, in the end, that "the passion for destruction, too, is a creative passion,"' he thought, as he remembered Bakunin subjectively; for he only saw those entombed in that sordid plane as sufferers of a kind of destruction—a tangible indictment of a society which condemns its own to the fringes, to the verge of cataclysm.

'What are you thinking?' asked Johnson, suddenly.

'Nothing.'

'Nothing is what you say when there is something,' he said, then continued, 'any road, whatever it is, you must bury it deep in your belly, even if for tonight only.'

Soon they reached the stall which was roofed with a tawny tarpaulin, parading a shoddy plywood nameplate with the inscription *Tochi's Food* in clear view and pillared by weather-beaten posts. Situated beneath the tarpaulin were a makeshift counter and food-warming containers and ancillary paraphernalia. Modest wooden benches flanked the counter for converging omnivores to sit and sate their famished guts. Although low-priced, the disrelish and hesitation with which The Nomad initially viewed the modest stall had over time yielded to its artisanal peculiarity. Now, his gullet basked in its bliss whenever fortune smiled on him directly or through Johnson. Indeed, he tucked ravenously into his double portions on that day.

'How was it?' Johnson asked, as his puckery face beamed with surfeit.

'It was alright. Thank you.'

The Nomad always felt grateful whenever Johnson came to his rescue as on this day, but he sometimes felt a rash of scorn for Johnson's constant benignity, which he thought emasculated him in some measure. He would often wish he could vanish into the brume of the Void, away from Johnson's benignities forever.

Shortly after they departed the stall for their next destination, the dusty potholed path reminded The Nomad again of Audoghast, where hills of granite road metal always sat unutilized by the roadside—forever suspended in the jiggery-pokery of unfinished pork-barrel undertaking—often to the anguish of commuters.

Johnson waved down a bike, the cheaper—and often the faster—mode of transport in many parts of Kangaba.

'Kangaba Lounge,' he said.

'No, wait,' said The Nomad as he pulled Johnson aside, confounded by what he'd heard.

'What do you mean Kangaba Lounge? You and I know too well, at least as you have often told me, that the place is a rip-off. So what is going on?'

'Well, of that they are guilty. But I never said I loathed being ripped-off under the right circumstances. Did I?'

'Don't be a thriftless, or shall I say, wooden-headed spender. I don't know how much you have won, but in sparingness, there is gain to be had. As we seldom do, let's go to the speakeasy and chug the heady rotgut instead.'

'See, uhh… Ogbeni, whatever we spend tonight at that strip club will not be ours. Fortune has showered its windfall on me, and now we must bask in its debauched ordinance. From the street it came, to the street, it shall return. Let's go! The rider is simmering with rage already.'

They straddled the pillion and departed for Kangaba Lounge.

3

Everything had happened very quickly. The Nomad had managed to extricate himself from the ghastly bedlam of the hecatomb, choosing to lodge in a rustic guest house, too knackered and too shaken to wend his way abode. In the backseat, unsettled and on the qui vive, The Nomad paid no heed to the garrulous cabby reeling off a shaggy-dog story as though his fare depended on it. From time to time, he would knuckle his eyes and snuffle aloud, though aware of his frantic state of mind: a nagging, intractable disquietude that seemed to represent a lot more than what had just happened, a subtle conveyor of something yet unknown, wrenching his guts to become hardened against the twists and torsions of a gnarly future.

At Adal Guest House—a gated, flaky-walled, double-storey entombed in outlandish vapidity and afflicted with a swaggering receptionist and a coterie of beer-bibbing cradle-snatchers and their pliable jailbaits who made his skin crawl—he would find out through a text from Remi, Ìgè's first wife, that her husband had been abducted by the regime's Gestapo at their home at the dead of night and had been possibly gaoled in one of the infamous, stockaded dungeons of the Gestapo. In the next breath, he would find out on the television news in his slight room the official statement of the Gestapo flagrantly confirming the abduction and describing Ige as a 'miscreant' who had 'breached public peace' in concert with others 'at large,' and ending with a list of those *others*, eight in total including The Nomad, all of whom were from Southern Audoghast, signalling the imprimatur of the high command.

He was, in a wink, assailed by a blast of high-strung emotions, bursting at once into a frenetic back and forth, pacing aggressively on the stone-coloured rug covering the floor of the room as though he were scuffling with a non-physical poltergeist—half-erratic, half-discomposed. In a tick, he reached out to Jerry, his long-time acquaintance and a chronic night-owl, narrated his predicament, and requested his assistance knowing he would be able to help.

'I need to disappear,' he had said to Jerry.

At a point in his life when all he could do were a string of odd jobs, The Nomad had met Jerry at Bushmen & Co., an international beverage company where they both worked and got along like two peas in a pod—the former as a janitor and the latter a steward. Unlike the other workers, however, Jerry was a deep-dyed bibliophile whose compelling devotion to the written word would, in time, permanently rub off on The Nomad. It was he who suggested that they enrol on Mr Vancock's World Literature part-time course, where The Nomad applied himself to studying Greek, Russian, French and the Great Saharan literature to a fault. Jerry thought The Nomad's preference for Tolstoy was indefensible, and The Nomad in turn found Jerry's obsession with Voltaire sickening, though they invariably agreed on the intellectual authority of illustrious Great Saharan writers, both for the content of their work and the supreme relatability they provoked in the mind of readers. Often, however, they were at an impasse over the likely surpassing quality of the literature written by Great Saharan women in comparison to those written by men, The Nomad taking a fierce position against such a sacrilegious argument, indeed the thought of it! Even if it were so, Jerry would reason once at his wits' end, was this not one of those questions that would forever split the lovers of literature into opposing halves?

Jerry, however, also had a weird bond with some of the terrifying fraternities in Southern Audoghast, details of which he occasionally shared with The Nomad who was mostly ambivalent about such matters. At any rate, their shared love of books would help sustain their acquaintanceship until that fateful night.

'I know some people. I will be in touch before 10 a.m., but I will send you a link to an encrypted platform where we can continue to talk. Don't phone me directly again.' Jerry said to him.

'Thank you, my good man,' he said to Jerry.

The next day, at exactly 10 a.m. when the sun had fully broken out of its sheathing and its scorching heat had begun to radiate a searing candescence over the surface of Southern Audoghast, Bode—one of the heavies of an underground network and the main man to a fraternal semblable of a friend of a friend of Jerry's—showed up at The Nomad's middling lair to superintend their manoeuvring of the Gestapo's dragnet. A scabby-faced, thick-lipped, brawny bloke with brownish teeth, Bode's visage was as intimidating as it was reassuring. He would go on to lay down the unexceptionable schema— from appearance and comportment to resources and projected expenses—for navigating the Daedalian labyrinth they must overmaster to get The Nomad to safety.

'We will for the most part move through the unplumbed byroads where our uniformed allies would resume their beats from 6 p.m. and we are likely to encounter little to no impediment,' said Bode, before he started off to tie up all loose ends.

. . . .

A grizzly sexagenarian beaming with unalloyed gratification was emerging from one of the rooms at the middling guest house, his left hand roosting cordially on the midsized rump of his burqa-wearing mistress when Bode and The Nomad strode past them, the latter passing a side glance over the trysters from underneath his baseball cap as if they were non-persons. "Shameless scumbag," he sniped at the odd fellow sotto voce.

Their journey to the southern border of Audoghast began in earnest after they had eased past the recursive roadblocks of grabby officers of the law—whose unvarying hymn was *Oga, anything for the boys?*—inveigling the duo to part with chump change at every point.

'We would have given up a lot more than that if we had travelled earlier in the day or followed the major road,' said Bode as they inched closer to the toilsome part of their 127-kilometre journey. The Nomad nodded the whole time like someone who had been hit by a life-reversing curveball. But the hardest part of their journey was the last 27 kilometres where the most rapacious and mean-spirited immigration checkpoints were coterminously embedded. And so, to bypass the mercurial micro-world of these bogeymen, they had planned to link up with Rosco—a lumberjack by day and fixer by night—at a pre-agreed rendezvous, which would also serve as their arcane pit stop for refreshments and vital organic functions.

Rosco, a broad-shouldered fixer with a distinct reputation in the underground network—his facial cicatrix, pitch-coloured eyelids and nimble deftness serving as his unique signature—led the way as the trio ploughed through a hazy wooded pathway, intricately circuitous and psychologically discomforting to The Nomad.

'No worry, my oga, we dey together. If anything show, I go cleave am like firewood,' said Rosco, revealing the hilt of his panga to The Nomad, which made the latter flinch interiorly but dissemble it just as quickly, as though any sign of vulnerability could prove fatal at that moment.

A flitting thought singed The Nomad's mind and he could not help but think, there and then, that that fugitive venture was probably the most fat-witted and disregardful decision he had ever made in his entire life. He was uncertain as to which was worse: navigating the spiderweb of petrified despotism or the fact of doing it through the perilous shoals of an underground ecosystem.

He knew something about that unnerving journey was quite momentous: it was unhidden to his faculties that his life was undergoing a process of frenetic transmutation, that he was not only ploughing through a strange woodland with half-trusted strangers but he was also ploughing through a tubercle of interlocked filaments, a plenum of hardened matter sown with self-generative and self-destructive fibres. He could tell that, in a way he had never experienced, there was a hard-edged sense in which his plodding and toiling through that fearful thicket shrouded in darkness was reshaping his existential reality, redefining its constitution and palpitations by giving it a new form in which the genie was now asserting itself—a sense of dangerous freshness that was emerging in sequence to a definite astral coagulation, a total rebirth of his daemon and material life force.

Meanwhile, a different alley was opening up ahead and the canopied woodland, spinose plants and thorns, wilting frondage, lengthy underbrush and clumps of obscure sprouts continuously thinned out towards a glade overlaid with chlorotic duff. Almost at the centre of the glade, a scraggy figure suddenly emerged from the infinite dimness like a bat out of hell, oozing the whiff of dread and the skulk of death; although he turned out to be Maku—Rosco's sallow-faced ally who only spoke in a sort of esoteric vulgate and helped The Nomad cross the frontier between Audoghast and the next country, Lomey, which was a buffer state between Audoghast and Tagaza, a prospering state endued with overflowing salt pans westward of Audoghast.

'Boss, just do anything him tell you and you go dey alright,' said Rosco to The Nomad as he and Bode bade their farewell.

Some minutes later, beyond the colonnade of blanched rookeries and nesting heronry, and the nerve-wracking sensations of crossing a deathly river in a rickety dugout propelled by rubber-plate sculls, The Nomad was finally on the other side of the frontier between Audoghast and Lomey, his primary concern then—among his litany of concerns—being the border patrolmen, all of whom Maku dealt with like a doddle one after the other.

From Lomey, The Nomad mapped out his hundreds of kilometres journey to Kangaba with Maku, setting out as soon as his plan was as taut as he thought would suffice to beat the transnational stoolies and syndics of Audoghast at their own game.

••••

Several months later, The Nomad's two thousand kilometres of peripatetic manoeuvring, venturesome uncertainties and gruelling daredevilry would melt away like lazy wind against the backcloth of statuesque pyrotechnics diffused over the asphaltic and cobbled streetscape of Upper Kangaba, and the stately parade of varicoloured, high-altitude structures aglow with tectonic magnetism and grandiose nullities. Each day in Upper Kangaba sucked him more and more into its sinkhole of gaudy vulgarities, its ostensible tranquillity and specious tridimensionality. In those early days, The Nomad grew fond of the little pleasures to be found in Upper Kangaba, exploring neglected historic castles and palaces, taking idle walks at night, grudgingly acquainting himself with and later swearing off upmarket eating houses and wine bars, sporadically indulging his fleshly pursuits, never fully involved with this or that, and occasionally keeping up with events back in Audoghast, his resentment and indifference taking a turn for the worse with the tedious passing of time.

Although he met Kiona during this period, she was determined to be no more than the lady who occasionally sent him affordable home-made meals, despite his persistent wheedling to turn her otherwise. 'I can't just leave him like that, you know,' she would say in response to The Nomad's wheedling, referring to her romantic partner whom he had decidedly exorcized to a distant orbit of facelessness. At first, The

Nomad assumed bedding Kiona would be nothing but a bludge, a straightforward conquest more or less, that all he had to do was patronize her long enough until the job was done. But with time, her unshakeable rejection of his persuasions made him maniacally obsessed with her, perceiving every portion of her fleshy form afresh and through magnified lenses, even the linear deep-set incisions on both sides of her face, the lasting scorn of a rigid tradition. Occasionally, they would caress and fondle and even spoon each other, but the actual experience which The Nomad feverishly desired was always a step too far to Kiona. The infatuation died on account of its own cost, The Nomad having reached the precipice of his financial desperateness.

By and by, after his first six months in Kangaba—twenty-one months to the day since he began his onward nomadic drift; for, indeed, he had stopped at multiple intervening states like Tagaza where he lodged in a moderate hotel for two months; in Takon where he rented a homette for three months and three weeks; in Sosso where he rented a bedsit for five months; and in Bono where he lodged in a middling guest house for two months and four days, before arriving in Kangaba three days later—he would admit that he had become a pipsqueak dwindling in a sandstorm of blinding distortion, a wadi bed battered by severe desiccation, a dingy wasteland enveloped by a filigree of false securities stifling his quenchless soul with droplets of water; a glamorized tastelessness that, in all honesty, made him think less and less of Audoghast but also reminded him of an irretrievable wholeness, a dizzy descension that felt absolute and unforgiving, a wasting away of his concrete sense of identity.

In six months, his resources had been sapped of security, his spirits sapped of buoyancy, his thoughts sapped of quality, and his very life sapped of critical juices. His assumptions that night when he eased into the glowing, citified Upper Kangaba—that he had finally arrived in the state that boasted the streets paved and fortified with gold, his nomadic *terminus ad quem* after fifteen months on the road—had been shattered to smithereens, if at all there were any residual fragments of that busted hope. In six months, his romantic idealization of Kangaba had faded as quickly as the frisson that vitalized it on his arrival. At that point, he had realized that if all else was dissimilar between Kangaba and Audoghast, there was one similarity that stuck out in defiance of any cosmetic gilt: their shared pigeonholing of humanity into two laminated contrivances to gratify unchastened sadistic impulses—that deliberate sundering of society into urbanized and ghettoized polarities to which, The Nomad would later admit, he had fallen victim in Kangaba and had accelerated his material degenerescence.

Alas, necessity would lunge The Nomad towards Niani and its environs in Lower Kangaba. Three months earlier, his first time in the area, he had embarked on an unplanned surveying on his way back from grudgingly discarding a good chunk of his effects for chump change, taking notes of Niani's crudities—its unpaved roads, anaemic monochromic bidonvilles, half-completed and neglected buildings covered with rusty metal roofs and folded single-lap roofing sheets, the several hands holding out a bowl or two in hopes of charitable handouts, the roadside buskers singing for their supper, and so on—and the aimlessness, the confusion, the convolutions and realness that made it look like the whole of humanity had been thrown en bloc into a broiling cauldron, which made it all so repulsive and so obscene. He had flinched, and his stomach had churned at the shuddering thought that he might as well end up there, that that was the part of Kangaba where he might have to put up for some time, for an undefined while.

He would return to Lower Kangaba three months later to relinquish his smartphone for a song, though it was enough to rent him a shabby place in Niani. The idea itself had seemed to him horrible at first, and even when by force of circumstance it slid into his puddle of considerations, it was down the rung on the list of his preferred options. But he had seen his own end at this point, and he knew he was not only falling apart, but he was also coming to the bad. Now how else, he thought, was a man on his tod to act nowadays, when he looks about him and there is no rewarding enterprise in which he can safely and profitably partake; when the odds of securing a decent employ are piled by the yard against the locals and triply so against a fugitive sojourner. Again and again, he chewed the cud on this and on the fact of his own simple efforts foraging a great many situations vacant and unannounced job vacancies there in Kangaba. It had all come to nought, and he couldn't deny it anymore.

Those inutile downer runs job-hunting in Kangaba had reminded him of his first job at Naphtha Bank, before the allure of working for Hassan suddenly reared its head out of the precious tun of serendipitous opportunities in Southern Audoghast. He was fresh out of college and had his head in the clouds, fancied himself gliding on the wings of youthful optimism to the mountaintops. He had started out as a bank clerk at Naphtha Bank, then notched up and became a junior manager, bravely taking on his onerous pigeon of subtle micromanagement of micro-level staff and implacable customers, until one of his likeable upper-crust customers offered him the opportunity to work for Hassan. It was during his time as junior manager at Naphtha Bank that The Nomad first met Ige, who had burst into the bank fuming at anyone with a name tag, greatly displeased with a dispense error which had left his bank balance in the altogether. In due course however, The Nomad's timely intervention became the seed for his eventual friendship with Ige, who would later introduce him to Lanlehin and Ajegbemi. The trio sealed their place in his heart when they insisted on joining him on the trip to his hometown for Mama Jebba's committal. Life is a series of knockdowns from which you must pull yourself up for your sake and the sake of others, they had said to him in different words.

And so when, in the harrowing fullness of time, he finally found himself up a gum tree of a totally different kind, one that threatened his downright homelessness in Kangaba, he couldn't afford to linger a minute to think on his feet and act. *It makes no odds anyway*, he had said before finally selling off the smartphone. He had come to harbour a subtle disregard for the gadget, for its deceptive comfort, its deluding worthfulness, its conspicuous materialist simplism and, in fine, its unconsoling albatross. But for all that, a rigid sombre feeling overcame him at the point of parting with the device and he couldn't help feeling self-reproachful for many days after.

Before that time, however, he still had a run-of-the-mill rented room in Upper Kangaba where—he would later admit after some time in Niani—the leaky air-conditioner and ink-wash painting on the ermined interior wall were the actual objects of import that offered him some sort of gratification in that glorified cubbyhole. Everything else—the 32-inch TV that he barely knew its display colours, the mini-refrigerator with which he frequently conspired to sustain his humdrum spells of boozing, the double-ring electric hob which sat mostly unused in its corner—diminished in significance, at irregular intervals, to the leaky air-conditioner and ink-wash painting.

The air conditioner gave him a sense of daily purpose: the tingling satisfaction he felt from fetching a bowl to collect the drips, the care he took in ensuring the bowl was well-placed, the little plops that made his heart stop for a teeny flitting second—those plops that made his stomach curl up, stiffen and slacken as though he had just guzzled a dram—the thimblefuls that nettled, pacified and consoled him all at the same time. It was those infinitesimal moments—amplified, no doubt, by the spiralling appeal of the several strains of tea introduced to him by Kiona—that made him feel as though he was truly living. The bizarre relish he derived from those moments, to some degree, convinced him that there was nary a need to pester the self-absorbed caretaker—he was doing just fine with the leaky air conditioner.

And then he had the ink-wash painting. It was one of those whimsies he never knew how to explain, but the painting had a way of peering into his soul, of burrowing into his inner crevices and calling forth his imaginative and facultative propensities. It had a life force that exuded ingenuity, that inspired endless kaleidoscopic imagery, that conjured intertextual antinomies, that glaringly exposed and sometimes effaced all tawdriness, that inspired nostalgia and susurrated otherworldly notions, that illumined a self-contained atomic mass and banished it into benightedness when it became too bright. For those who had declared it impossible, he would sometimes say to himself, they must study this painting as the result of a fruitful conspiracy between man and djinn, artist and spirit. In his soliloquies, The Nomad would insist the painting was a victim of disrespected perfection which did not deserve its tacky frame. It deserved no less than a golden frame. Then he would sometimes think it was all part of the art. That this thing called art was, after all, the freedom to confound and stupefy.

But Muniruk—his doughy, hard-bitten, middle-aged caretaker—was not so artfully inclined. He was as thorny as acacia. It was probably his failure as a blacksmith that made him so unfeeling. It was he who—with his puckered face one morning, and his foul-smelling harmonica chain dangling above his scoop-neck t-shirt—gruffly expelled The Nomad from Upper Kangaba three weeks after the latter failed to renew his rent.

PART 2

Mo ja'we igbegbe
Ki won ma gbagbe mi
Mo ja'we oni tete
Ki won ma te mi m'ole

I plucked the leaves of gbegbe
Lest I be forgotten
I plucked the leaves of tete
Lest I be trodden under

—Wole Soyinka
Of Africa

4

Kangaba Lounge ravelled itself out to a slopy descent as a three-storey aubergine edifice, environed by high-rise structures and rebarbative buildings, about five and a half kilometres from The Nomad's foxhole in Niani. The outer walls were burnished with silvery distemper and daubed with suspicions of aureate hues, glimmering under the luminance of animating floodlights.

The topmost floor was bifurcated by sliding folding partitions bespeckled with glistening polka dots and curlicues: the dextral wing was reserved for prominent dives and prodigal politicians while the sinistral was always for standard roisterers. Beneath that sky-proximal floor was a mezzanine where the saloon bar glistered like vitrified chestnuts, where divers indoor activities found unhindered expression: logoed billiard tables carpeted with lilac and vermilion baizes on one side; table tennis, cup pong, step quoits and dartboards in sectioned cubicles, on the other—teeming with varied gamesters and topers.

On the ground floor there were tough-faced, beardless, muscled bouncers standing sentry and wielding transceivers, flanked by soft-spoken damsels in custom-made monogrammed shirts and shell-pink brooches, verifying entry cards of prominent dives and handing out wristbands to standard roisterers. The bannisters leading from one floor to the next glowed with bawdy inscriptions twinkling in calligraphic modes on the interior walls—*PUMPUM SUKUTUM, LICKITY-JIGGIDY, BADDIES ONLY, etc., etc.*—so that as roisterers ascended and descended the staircases, they were reminded that Kangaba Lounge was the home of debauchery. On the standard wing of the topmost floor, which seemed like an explosion in a paint factory for its prismatic coruscation, there was more than enough to alter the flurried mind of The Nomad to match Johnson's scrutable zestfulness.

'Amazing, right?' asked Johnson, his hands sheathed in his jean pockets and his shoulders beaming with the pride of a pleasure-seeker.

The Nomad nodded his head vaporously, leaving Johnson confused on whether he nodded in agreement or as an abstracted relator of their bubbly atmosphere.

They ploughed through the boisterous human concentration proximal to the entrance and made towards a vacant seat at the relatively hole-and-corner nook of the septenary loungescape. A thin on top, stocky, pliant-seeming fellow with a satchel strapped to his funnel chest like a sash approached them to take their order and returned soon after with a 750ml Lambrusco frizzante with a glittering capsule, while the banging music declined briefly for an accompanying hearse-fitting rhapsody.

'Bah! They didn't have to do that,' The Nomad piped up as the page, Martins—according to the schematic name stamp on his chest—left them to their own devices.

'What now?' asked Johnson, looking rather exercisable.

'They didn't have to stop the music or even play that rhapsody. Those bells and whistles are better reserved for swanks and attention-seeking worldlings.'

'That's conventional practice at any club like this. It is as much a marketing strategy as it is an ego-boosting thing for the customer. Any road, I am sure you know that.'

'I do, but never have I been comfortable with such vainness. They should at least ask if some persons do not wish to be perceived as vaunters, or have their ethical core assailed by needless frivolousness.'

Johnson shrugged, then outstretched his hands to do the drinks, making sure their glasses were charged, fizzling with bubbles of sparkling mousse.

At the peak of its existence, Kangaba Lounge was still unrivalled in all of Lower Kangaba on the night the duo made their way there, for the reason that it offered more than the usual that was obtainable in other nightclubs—a concatenation of sensuous women diverting a voyeuristic audience. Settled in their cushiony sofa, the duo would realize they had occupied a vantage from which their eyes had become synoptic witnesses to rigidly rivetted dance poles of about fourteen feet on which a salad of semi-disrobed strippers performed one after the other, as neon-lit flickers nictated rapidly and without end.

It was not the snake-hipped stripper who, in truth, snaked remarkably on the winding pole that won The Nomad's attention—though she did win Johnson's and lapped up his attention awhile. Neither was it the wooden display by the crotchless stripper who made an inanimate show after her. Nor was it the posey, ringleted dancer whom The Nomad thought must be avoided for unspecific reasons, and her rather scrawny partner, whose overly flaunty display crossed The Nomad as too artificial.

Rather, it was the dark-skinned stripper with distinct carmine hair, whose sense of self-regard radiated from her supple gait and vivid deportment, that engraved a pleasurable impression on The Nomad's mind. Soon, he was basking in the serendipity of watching her splendacious striptease.

'Between you and me, that girl is immaculate,' The Nomad chirped suddenly, in a slightly stentorian rap to Johnson.

'Hahaha, really?'

'Of course! This is what we call a finely made specimen. Can't you see?'

'Take it easy now. You don't even know if she gives a fig about you. Here is a general truth for you: In a strip club you will only find queans, never queens.'

'Bilge! There is nothing to suggest she is a badly behaved one, neither is there any truth to your time-worn factoid. These are special creatures borne of the same world to which you and I belong, to fault their line of work is to make a futile rail against the involved scope of being human. As a matter of fact, I now feel strongly about getting to know her.'

'No crime in that. But don't say I did not warn you: beware of these femme fatales,' Johnson said, in a rather fatidic tone.

The satchel-hugging page, Martins, returned with two pieces of tea, specially ordered by Johnson, a sighting for which the latter disposed of his tube's fag end immediately. 'This is the real deal,' Johnson said, as he passed one to The Nomad.

'In a sense, are they not all the real deal?' The Nomad queried.

'Well, maybe. But I can tell you this is very different; even old hands struggle with it, still less first-timers. Any road, I know you have always held your own.'

In no time, however, a sudden sensation began to assume a drifty form in The Nomad's mind, an uprush that seemed to have accompanied the tea he had just received and was pulling on lightly. He could not, at first, explain what he was feeling, for it was a dizzying anomaly that impaled like a rush of formication, a sudden wind of apprehension which seemed to amaze and unsettle him at once. *How the most conspicuous things could sometimes escape a person's realm of consciousness and then sneak freely back into that realm as if they had always been there, as if they never even left!*—he thought. Surely there must be something about being there at Kangaba Lounge, in the flesh, at that moment? A privilege or indication of a preordained process?—he queried, examining the merits of this point and other grist besides. Indeed, it was the most obvious things that had brought The Nomad to this place of passing reflection: the simple busyness of his milieu, the endless alterations of forms and social togs, the switching of faces and layers of interactions; voyeurs, carousers, gigglers and thigh-slappers changing places like freckled husks peeling off in obedience to some deathless factor. He looked at each of them as they departed and arrived like ambulating weather patterns, each wearing on his dial diametrically conflicting expressions.

Were those discontent, anticipation and gratification rolled into one composite experience?

Then it suddenly occurred to him that everyone, everything in that lounge, must be serving an end that transcended any human design and scheme the mind might ever conceive. In his mind's eye, it seemed plausible that they were all playing out a sequenced role in some Byzantine planetarium, each compelled by an inviolable injunction to give to all that the lounge had to offer and equally receive from its generous cauldron. A quid pro quo geared toward catapulting the soul into the sublime. These other carousers, he thought, represented a peculiar experience—jugglers of the tactile and the abstract; there they were, himself included, gormlessly instantiating a chasing and a fleeing of a concrete condition. A chasing and fleeing, it would seem, of the harlequin decomposition that essentializes the human experience—not knowing whether or not their sequenced performance had a predetermined upshot which may fecundate as it may well frustrate the yearnings vegetating deep in their souls.

—'Ogbeni,' Johnson called out suddenly, his broad thighs and limbs playing congenial hosts to Rashida, the gracile stripper who had lapped up his attention earlier.

'Yes?'

'You seem distracted...'

'Oh, no. I am just amazed by how she is able to do that flawlessly,' replied The Nomad, his gaze cast on the graceful stripper who, in his mind, seemed to be moulded from the cancan sort of the Moulin Rouge. Her spirality and whippiness on the pole, unbeknownst to him, had considerably, if not totally, dissolved his vestigial melancholy.

Although unintended, The Nomad had become somewhat infatuated as he revelled in the swivelling pole on which his object of fancy fascinated him—him alone, as he now thought—far more than the other roisterers. He remained enraptured in his infatuation, though also mulling over the imagined pleasure of reseeding his scorched pockets—the satisfaction of simply having enough, not necessarily much, to lavish freely. In relative clover, he thought, the slurry pit of beggarly hands would be a reality of the yonder, and temperance would grovel at the feet of his bacchanalian proclivities.

But suddenly, his starry-eyed thoughts began to transmogrify into timbres of crystallizing fancies, unfolding with such unignorable intensity which made him nonplussed, momentarily stark and deadpan in countenance all at once. He could tell from the observatory in which he was niched, that in the way they both espied and ogled each other with what seemed a curious and intentional longing, no stentorious impulse on either side could derail the endpoint of the unwinding process; an end which he could see tilting towards a certain bight which he could not wait to experience. He had conjured up and assayed a mélange of fancies and oddities, considered all and any worthwhile arrow in the quiver: a strictly lumber-esque dalliance just to have his end away—to which he was only mildly inclined, the good sense or folly of a disinterested façade, and so on. Yet, he felt like he was being smouldered by this unresolved puzzle—tinged, it seemed, with the likelihood that he was about to bungle it all. Perhaps he would have to duck and dive this one...

'Hello,' the fruity voice echoed down to the entrails of The Nomad, and indiscernible sensations fretted across his palms.

'Hello,' he responded, instantly reaching out with a cosy and eager handshake. Flurries of vaporous emotions sizzled his soul as he essayed to make way for the smiling damsel.

Johnson, inscrutable in his suspect but smile-spliced stare, now tilted his broad thighs in an attempt to make room for the lavendered damsel sidling up to The Nomad, the latter's face blooming with transports of ravishment.

'I will be back,' Johnson said as he and Rashida made towards the pavilion to shroud each other in the brine of dissolution.

'Drink?' asked The Nomad, motioning the frizzante on the mauvish buffet stool.

'Yes, please.'

The Nomad, with a poorly dissembled amatory smile, gazed at the lady's lustred zippered dress, his face travelling down to her see-through fishnet, only to return to her dimpled fizzog, which made his body pullulate with lust.

'You know, I wasn't sure whether to stay or scram when you were approaching me,' he said, as he passed her a half-filled glass.

'Really? Am I not much to look at?'

'Oh, no. No, please. It's not that at all. I guess I was in two minds about my ability to keep it together, or to at least not bungle your coming to me.'

'I see. There is no reason to feel that way though. I thought to come over since our eyes met many times while I was on the dance pole.'

'Yes, yes. You are right. Funnily, I did not intend for that to happen. I must have been looking at you for a while.'

'I am sure it was more than a while,' she said as they both let out a relaxed laugh.

'I am Cynthia, but my friends call me Brownshuga.'

'Oh! Brownshuga. I like that. You can call me Ogbeni, though I should add that I don't have a sobriquet.'

'What?' asked Cynthia, leaning sideways towards The Nomad's lips, trying to pick up what he was saying as the sudden loudness of the music threatened to eclipse their choked voices.

'Sorry, I said my name is Ogbeni, though I must warn you I don't have a fancy nickname.'

'Oh. Ogbeni. That is a weird name.'

'Is it?'

She bobbed her head in affirmation.

'I don't know why it feels clumsy—so don't ask me why. But, it's a pleasure to meet you, Mr… Ogbeni.'

'It's a pleasure to meet you too, Cynthia—sorry, Brownshuga.'

'Would you like me to give you a lap dance?'

'Err… ahem, excuse me. I think that would be nice. But, can we talk a little before that?' he faltered.

'Sure. As long as you pay me, you can talk to me till morning.' Cynthia said, seeming to laugh as The Nomad dissembled his sudden queasiness with a tentative laugh as well.

'Why do you look like that?'

'How now?'

'Don't you want to pay me?'

'That's not it.'

'Then what?'

'I have just been thinking about you differently since I set my eyes on you.'

'Oh, please. Don't be one of them. You all say that a lot; it has become deadly dull.'

'Well, I suppose you have a point there. And it isn't our fault either: you are a beautiful woman that would make any man crow at first sight.'

'Hahaha. That's new.'

'Well, it's from the depths of bottomless truths.'

In response, a dainty smile fleeted across Cynthia's facial outline, as she led her left hand like trained ramblers to feel the rigidly formed phallus that cemented itself to The Nomad's left thigh.

'No woman will have this at her whim, and ever deem herself unlucky.' She said, spunkily.

'Really?' asked The Nomad, slightly diffident.

'I am sure of it.'

'You are too kind.'

Soon, she chucked her voluptuous form on his thighs, making sure his phallic line remained glued to her crack, and sank his partially wasted face in the cleavage sundering her plump bosom, girding and chafing his temples fondly with the globes, then she brushed his lips with her areola and caulked his mouth with her teats as if to surfeit him with nectar.

'I like you,' she whispered breezily in his ears, rendering The Nomad both excited and discombobulated.

Wow. Is that what she says to everyone or am I the first? Is this a kind of game in which I am supposed to momentarily doff my discerning hat and act like an unthinking automaton? Perhaps I should seize the chance to ask her pointedly: 'Do you truly like me or do you just want to lead me down the garden path?' No. That's too soppy. It is probably too early to say anything like that. But she might be waiting to hear that from me... No matter, I will content myself by believing I have not completely lost my Byronic charm—the reason for which, I hope, she had said that to me in the first instance.

'Really?' he asked shortly after.

'Yes. Do you like what I'm doing now?' she whispered again, gently stroking her crack against the bulbous phallus between his legs, the orifice crowning his hopeless meatus dripping tiny amounts of sticky fluid.

'Yes. It's just unbelievable how you do it so well. You are amazing,' he whispered back in response.

A brief ticking of seconds and Cynthia said peremptorily: 'Come. Let's go to my room.'

He was stumped and intrigued: *The tone. That's a tone I would beg for. I was right to be fixated on this one. She has got the guts; I want all that comes with that and more.* He muttered in his mind, as a wicked smile irradiated his visage.

Those imperious words from Cynthia became ramified in The Nomad's thoughts as he fantasized and at the same instant, ruminated over what the potential issue of such a move would be for him, considering all things—including and especially financially. The sketches singed his brain like the deuce, but his innate acumen seemed to have escaped him without warning. He felt as though his thinking parts had fallen into abeyance— he wished to stop and think, but he found himself somehow determined against such stultifying and pretentious nonsense.

The urge to follow unquestioningly had chucked him against Cynthia's rump, and for the first time, bottle and wineglass in hand, he thought he had a perfect view of her glorious rump; and the more he stared, the more engrossed he got. Gradually, the visible gave way to the tangible, and the tangible ushered in the olfactorily perceptible: all his senses seemed to have become hyperactive; he could not only see, but he could also feel and perceive Cynthia's erotic appeal. Then they egressed through a claret-coloured door which led, apparently, to the pavilion which Johnson and Rashid had earlier departed for. Every pace forward left a palpable diminuendo in their wake. Before long, they were plunged into a curious abysm.

For a brief moment, the emptiness felt like stasis in a Stygian crypt, impenetrable and frozen. Then, Cynthia flicked the switch and The Nomad's hypothalamus flipped with it—his interior wiring was instantly swallowed by volcanic sensations, and he felt himself skirting the margins of decadent descent as the last parapet of continence within him began to recede and fall apart like clockwork. Cynthia, nay, Brownshuga, had become to The Nomad the avatar of Aphrodite; her form had become the conveyor of soul-stirring rhythms, and her lickerish gaze had begun to ravish him like an all-consuming narcotic. She made towards him, like a philistine sorceress determined to steer his crescentic fantasies.

'Give me your hand,' she said, fluttering her eyelashes, as she led him to the fleecy quilt covering the rubbery mattress encased in a locally made bed leaning against the wall.

Randy pinups, friezes and traceries of unbounded earthiness coated in patchy emerald and amethyst mosaic overlaid the neon-dappled wall. The windows were visibly frosted from the chilly air-conditioning, and the entire four-walled encasement, to an extent, felt like a fated attempt at self-renewal. He inhaled and exhaled pleasurably, then waved his head from side to side, as if he had just been hit by some hard-nosed reality. Indeed, he was astonished by his own reaction and train of thought. He concluded there and then that the form of a man's life is like the barbed edges of a brier; for, even in reduced circumstances, lechery tugged at his sleeves.

Suddenly, Brownshuga shoved him to the bouncy bed and followed him slinkily. Then she sat beside him and held his left hand, running her fingers across the uneven prints on his palm.

'You have a beautiful hand,' she said softly.

'Ha ha, I see you've got some humour, and your mouth is pure mutton—gooey and sweet. I wonder, is that part of the business?'

94

'What more is there to say than the truth which can be seen? Your hand betrays no known hardship, it is fine and soft to the touch—and your smile makes you attractively mysterious. Or...' She looked him in the eyes and asked, 'are you now in a hurry to get down to it?'

'Um, not really. No doubt, there is an undeniable babelicious energy around you and this... this mini sanctum you have brought me. But, I am not like those men who rush their pleasures.'

Smiling mystically, she responded, 'Hmm. That's good. Your hand... this hand in particular'—pointing her index finger to The Nomad's left hand and peering into his palm—'is making me curious. May I read your palm?'

The Nomad, thinking nothing serious of this and chuckling like a good-timer enslaved by reckless infatuation, nodded affirmatively.

'You may go ahead,' he said.

'I am serious.'

'I am serious too! Ha ha.'

'You must think I am joking. But palmistry is part of me and I am part of it. It is like second nature to me.'

'See, I don't believe in such things, so don't let us waste time dwelling on it.' The Nomad said, seeing now that she was becoming quite distracted.

'Perhaps,' he added, quite queerly, 'you should go ahead and *read my palm*,' he drawled sarcastically.

'Good. Very good.' She said, quite enthusiastically as she adjusted her posture, leaving a luscious bit of her pendulous bosom to titillate The Nomad, as though she wanted him to bury whatever was left of his senses in it.

'Okay. Are you ready?' she asked.

'Whenever you are.'

Within a brief interval, her gaily expression turned glum and sober.

'What is it?' The Nomad asked.

'I think this is wrong. We should stop.'

'But you started it. Now that our feet are in the water—feet we ushered into this water deliberately, I must add—I think a plaint of cold would be most unnatural. Now say what you must and let us get it over with.'

'Okay. If you insist.'

'I insist.'

'Well then. I can see you are in the rough and floundering in a battery of auguries. I can see it will remain so for some time to come. But, I can also see this: that if you pray to your gods to toughen you with resilient fortitude against the tortures of life, that even if your bones decay in formaldehyde, they will yet rise as a whole and in the pink again.'

There was palpable silence for a minute or two, and Cynthia's face glinted cloddishly in tints of greasy smiles. The Nomad's aspect betrayed nothing but his flinty glazed expression.

Then, in a trice, he rose to his feet, stood akimbo and snorted for a moment, then trudged back and forth, intermittently looking daggers at Cynthia, before storming off. His feet moved with a fiery temper as he rushed out to nowhere in particular, then stopped suddenly amidst the ruck of roisterers at the strip club, his bloodshot eyes flashing about as if intent on spotting unseen darts. Then, in a split second, his grimace softened as he saw Johnson and walked up to him sardonically, although the latter was visibly occupied with a different stripper whose thigh-opening glommed on lusciously to his priapic outline. As he approached them a sudden feeling overwhelmed him, eerie and unnatural to his marbles. He tried to choke back the feeling but it only ballooned monstrously.

'Ogbeni!' Johnson exclaimed on seeing The Nomad again, 'I have asked around for you. I understand you have been attending to something around the corner, ha ha.'

'It's nothing, or it turned out to be nothing at least,' he retorted with a long face.

'What happened?'

'It's nothing to bother about,' he said, and paused. 'Well,' he continued, 'I just wanted to check in with you. I will be back soon.'

'Sure. You have all the time in the world my man. Ha ha.'

And in a fit of hardly suppressed rage, The Nomad nodded his head and turned around as his feet briskly departed Johnson's corner and made for the door to the strip club.

He was now fully out of temper and made no visible attempt to dissemble the fact, although he could not, in truth, explain why. He ploughed through the ruck and took no conscious notice of the marquee which had been erected outside, to divert roisterers who preferred or could only afford to be there. Not knowing whether to turn left or right outside, he felt inclined to hoof it and continued without looking back, walking in brusque and quicksilver paces in search of nothing, although he had the mien of one who was in search of something—now eager, now askance.

••••

The unpaved stretch took him down a winding road along a jagged, partly ballasted path enchaining a parade of idle retail stores, boutique booths and mini-malls, which preceded a three-way intersection. And then his feet marched hazily along an unfamiliar dirt road, shaped like a parabola, on which a derrick stood dauntingly, only a few miles before a well-known retirement home, Boskopoid; and on he went with the attitude of one walking towards a decided destination, or to a stamping ground.

As he marched on, his faculties were suddenly ambushed by the preceding scene at the strip club, so that he became downright incensed over what he perceived at that moment as a needless reaction to the pretentious nonsense of a feminine Tartuffe, disgorged from the bowels of his nonobvious antagonists. The more he walked, the more he felt the waves of fury piercing through his capsule, riling his soul from within.

I should have said something. I shouldn't have let her get away with that. If anyone ought to inflame me like this, she should not have been the one—no, not in this way. I should have known when I saw her donning the hair of an orang-outang. And why in the world am I even distressed that someone on the game uttered utter crock to me! Nothing about that was serious in the first place. Or was it the way she said it? Do I feel guilty for letting her say that to me? Why? Why bother with such bollocks? It was all bluff. Bluff! Bluff! he griped without pause as he marched on like a peevish automaton.

The gentle midnight wind wafted through his body and whizzed around his ears as he burst forth in a soliloquy, examining what he should and should not have said, what he should and should not have done. He considered returning to the strip club just to scream in Cynthia's face and confute her plastic clairvoyance—to tell her how wrong she was and how anyone could have said exactly what she said, because of its meaninglessness, and how he, in particular, could have flung what she said back in her face without any fleck of remorse or cunctation.

But, in an instant, a rational voice from his silent interiority alerted him to a possible correspondence between Cynthia's palm-reading and his material reality. He shuddered from this inward nudge that she was perhaps not entirely wrong, that she was perhaps not wrong at all. And no sooner had his mind begun to consider this than he began to feel drawn to a curiously irresistible sight: A grove along his path had halted him in his track and, without rhyme or reason, he felt like it was the familiar camphor trees and saplings at the tip of the cul-de-sac back in Southern Audoghast.

There was no cask, neither was there guanacaste, but he felt like he had reached a familiar ground where he could slob around, even if for a brief moment. And, like the wind, he made close-grained pasteboard with shed leaves on which he sat and soused himself in the drones of geckos and praying mantis. Soon, gusts of epiphanous wind winnowed back and forth as he suddenly realized, for the first time since he left the strip club, that he had been wandering about unfamiliar roads and was now roosting under a grove far away from his original path. And just in that instant, a tenebrous feeling descended on him, followed by a languorous breeze that doused his curious mind as he reclined against the trunk and drifted off almost immediately.

5

A skyline of unmoving impenetrable objects unrolled itself to The Nomad along a dreary path as he clomped his way upland atop a stony ground interspersed with motes of dust and offscourings, which his spent feet scuffed up intermittently. His ponderous, slitted eyes gaped and shut at irregular intervals sighting a battery of curios that, in reality, were rude simulacra of terraced cubiform buildings along his fabulous gorge-seeming path. Undistinguished sounds of nature swished past his ears as he wobbled past overhanging jacaranda with full subliminal takes and retarded celerity.

Unridden steeds caparisoned with fetching trappings meshed into lucent forelocks of dusky manes cantered off in graceful gaits, trailed in his view by roaring streams abreast a drove road and interlinked with outcrops of dodgy monoliths, cypresses, hollies and shrubberies. Then a concatenation of lianas outstretched like limpets lining birches and fluffy baneberries rimmed the bourns of an interminable flatland spread out in his sight like an impeccably fearful patchwork. He luxuriated in the Elysian variegation and crooned to its idyllic sweep, playing his hands unguardedly like a stubby short of a sixpack, drifting in palpable nothingness, unbothered by the mundane concerns of unreality.

An embodiment of the Confucian wisdom 'when the mind is not present, we look and do not see; we hear and do not understand.' His legs suddenly hit a hillock of nebulous leavings, but he merely lolloped forward like a common dormouse. He slipped in his footing without notice as he plunged into a slough, fording and rustling through his clustered path as though on the cusp of grasping an entrée to the empyrean. He trawled his draggled feet along rank reeds and forged through unflustered.

But nothing in his unbroken somnambulism suggested the magnitude of his distending degenerescence, nor the unreality of his reality. To his eirenic mind, the scenic span was an Arachne meshwork of eidetic spectacle, laid out in skeins of immaculate tonalities to be relished to the nines. He was delightfully lodged in the dreamlike state in which he felt himself coursing through the boulevards of nirvana, although ripples of the moving lake and the pebbled shoreline betrayed a different reality.

Furious squeaks and flaps flittered above his head as he trudged down the narrow bank towards the pebbly shore and plunged his legs into the lake, until he was wading obliviously in springtime temperateness. Gradually, he began flailing about on fading footholds, teetering on the edge of overbalance and abruptly sinking until he was out of his depth. His clenched hands sprang out spasmodically with fistic jabs in fits of unconscious struggles, as gouts of gory fluid trickled over the surface of the lake from his occiput.

Suddenly, indistinct throats penetrated the acoustics span of his somnambulant subspace, howling in frantic sonority 'Arakunrin! Arakunrin!' The Nomad's mind abruptly and partially summoned from wool-gathering to reality, to his respiratory frontiers caving in, his hypoxic suffocation and instant pallidity suggesting he was then at the mercy of Olokun.

For a while he gasped for air, mumbling some indistinct words as his breath rapidly thinned out like dying cinders.

'Hurry! Nothing must happen to him. Olokun has declared his rescue from the talons of death.' This was Baba Faleke, bidding his sedulous acolytes Farounwi and Fagbami to scurry to the rescue of the drowning man as they halted their quarterly predawn rite. In a flash, Fagbami fetched a rustic Dafuna-like dugout from the dry dock by the shore and ushered it to the lake after which Farounwi, oaring through the riplets in a dither, paddled towards The Nomad, whose left hand peeked out lifelessly above the void. Baba Faleke watched on with bated breath, jiggling his rattle staff in hand and muttering empowered speech intermittently:

'You must live. Yes, you shall live. Your death is forbidden now.'

• • • •

A bald-headed, round-faced, unbearded, middle-aged widower of stout form and average height, Baba Faleke's devotion to the infinite arcana of traditional spirituality, sanative essentiality, even cosmic wholeness known as Ifá had made him a revered personage in his backwater community in Cannah—about seventeen kilometres from Kangaba Lounge and twenty-five from Niani.

Like the 'folded necks' of Cameroon whose habits betrayed as garish toffs, Baba Faleke's lifestyle only accentuated his status as a modest personage living in clover, having earned himself the status of a man of means when he worked as Head Factor for multiple multinational companies, before fully devoting himself to the boundless phenomena of Ifá. But unlike those whose greed precede their means—whose affinity for short-changing the weak, bludgeoning the strong, deuddering the exchequer, peculating, appropriating and committing rapine, only to later erect battlements to surveil their dirty pickings and shield their loot—at the heart of Baba Faleke's means stood an exemplary man of virtue.

As the only son of Awoshina, the great Ifá priest of Cannah, his acceptance of his ancestral obligation to serve Ifá and illumine the path of others was as easy as pie, an obligation which he gave alacritous expression from juvenescence. His self-willed devotion, his natural aptitude for Ifá's corpus, and his widely regarded mastery over the spirits of clairvoyance had carved him a good name among Ifá priests and even the laity, making him a first-choice Babalawo or votarist of the Ifá oracle to pilgrims wanting spiritual unriddling, or simply guidance on how to plod through the twisted web of life.

Soon, the rescuers were paddling the ebb and flow insusceptible to undertows, conveying The Nomad to where Baba Faleke stood in his all-white raiments, his sashed shoulders gravid with mystical energy beneath his vanishing neck. In the intervening period, the void is unsteadily pierced by dewdrops, settling on unfeeling pores like spittle in the wind. But in Baba Faleke's mind, he knew the will of Olokun is often enwrapped in bales of mystery; to understand, even the initiated must sip from the dew of calm and peace.

Now asprawl and unconscious in the dugout, the two acolytes, having exerted all their physical strength and deftness to get the unknown man out of water, watched The Nomad with palpable disquiet—tight-lipped, bulging eyes, throbbing breasts; their edginess belying the tranquil oozing from the lake as it laved the shore. Suddenly, the rescuers charged with fret towards the unconscious man, who was soaked through and frozen, attempting a sort of confused palpation and percussion on the non-swimmer. But a sudden dash bobbed the dugout up and down as if to make it keel over, causing Farounwi to swiftly awaken his dormant oars.

'O di eewo[3],' muttered Fagbami.

At the dell where Baba Faleke stood, a few inches from the shingle bounds, the acolytes in a dither set about to revive The Nomad. Like a drowned rat, The Nomad's skin was glued to the swarded ground, Farounwi's palm heels compressing his chest, while Fagbami in parrot-fashion backed Baba Faleke as he cantillated verses from the fitting Odu, their atmosphere mantled in mystic sombreness. Concurrently, Baba Faleke plucked clumps of sundry herbage from his chalky jute bag and made a poultice which he passed to Fagbami who stanched the gory seepage dribbling down The Nomad's occiput.

'You must live. Yes, you shall live. Your death is forbidden now.' Baba Faleke repeated his empowered speech.

'Ase,' chorused Fagbami and Farounwi.

One spurt after the other, The Nomad coughed up mouthfuls of water.

Groggy and merely half-conscious, The Nomad peered around him through his slitted eyes like one who had awakened to a strange world choking with strange faces. 'Can you see this?' asked Farounwi, who wagged his index finger to and fro, to ascertain The Nomad's state of consciousness.

---

3   Such is forbidden.

But at this point, his bloodless scowl had become a simulacrum of the infernal Darvaza gas crater. His unplanned slip through the doorway of the living had been just as well to him, but the sudden intrusion by Baba Faleke and his acolytes had merely invalidated that inward fancy, which he had subterraneously harboured before that fateful moment. Even if a man lacks many things—The Nomad would sometimes reflect in his brown study—he should be guaranteed the right to self-freeing. *This should at least be a universally imprescriptible human right, it should be legal anywhere insofar as there are humans who breathe and live there*—he once declared during his pensive spells. But this unsought intrusion had disregarded that subtle yen; yet again, he thought, aliens had conspired with life to deny him the privilege of self-gratification.

More than anything, the message he wished he had managed to leave behind—that he was gone at last to the world beyond, untethered to the dreariness of that world no more—had suffered the fatality of non-expression. And just as quickly, that flame fizzled out and The Nomad passed out there and then.

'Oya! Let's move him to Ile Ayo,' Baba Faleke bade his acolytes at once. The Nomad was quickly whisked on Farounwi's back, his undemanding weight hardly a strain on the latter's spine as they started off for Ile Ayo, a distance of only one mile and a half.

Spry and fleet-footed, Farounwi charged his legs with rapid haste while Baba Faleke and Fagbami trailed behind with as much speed as their feet allowed. The dawning day, morning haze, wilting shrubs, bird's-foot trefoils, arched lemongrass, and so on hardly made an impression on their flurried nerves. Nor did the dumpy woman bearing a hessian sack on a roundly moulded scarf balanced on her head, who greeted both men in a familiar dialect, cause a remarkable shift in mood—though she was well-responded to, given the circumstance.

As they drew nearer to Ile Ayo, Baba Faleke's multipurpose dwelling, the haze seemed to emerge thicker so that Fagbami almost tripped up when his right foot hit a mound of draff on their murram track. 'Be careful,' said Baba Faleke, as the bottom tip of his rattle staff pinched the ground sporadically, trailed by instant jingles of jin-win-rin-rin.

6

A stone paving of clastic rocks and slabs of hardened gravel overlaid the ground surface of Ile Ayo's forecourt; the domain itself was expansive and the preceding ground was a pathway of about nine feet wide, bordered on both sides by ramified ferns, hedgerows, and scattered beds of lifeless grass.

For a man of his status, Baba Faleke's forecourt was neither preceded nor succeeded by any iron barrier, save the ignorable wicket at the entrance of the red-brick pied-à-terre for novitiates, which was only a few yards from a row of alcoves along the sinuous veranda. Areca palms, chamomiles, vermillion cacti, pygmy date palms and several other plant varieties of stylar magnificence jutted out of terracotta pots, with a few well-crafted symmetrical planter benches collocated along the same stretch. These were followed in view by a scandent hydrangea and trellised ramblers, rolling sinistrally towards the portico. On the other side of the veranda, separated by the arcaded portico—hollowed up like a giant bumbershoot—was a wooden outdoor chaise lounge, spotting an oblong-shaped cushion of nitid velour. And adjoining the veranda was a puncheon flooring skillion or lean-to, covered by a deep aquamarine awning and housing a wattled pestle and mortar, sitting beside a sizeable volcanic stone molcajete, along with grinding stones and pipkins of several shapes and sizes. At the centre of this background were two rattan chairs, only a few yards from the sturdy wooden stools on the extreme end. Rows of floating shelves overlaid with kaross set out an omnium gatherum of herbs—including, inter alia, wormwood, medlar leaves, medlar rind, ground myrrh, varieties of nightshades and artemisia, and some anthelminthic bark, forming a tapestry of sectioned sanative spread.

There was, also, a small-scale cabinet containing wooden dishes, a plump beaded jute bag, some shiny treen and several tenebrous supplements. Followed by some carvings and figurines on plinths, all wooden and marvellously chiselled. And then, girthing the skillion all round and sloping laterally was a splendid spectrum of henna trees, canna lilies, rufescent geraniums, markhamia, gardenia, Warburgia ugandensis, bay laurel, basswood, walnut, and pine conifers, all bursting with vegetational verve and reflecting the imbibition of natural phenomena. The melodious trills of perched passerines, including swallows and thrushes, filtered through the atmosphere as the must gradually evaporated.

Inside, in a previously unoccupied room, The Nomad was barely conscious, his former state had given to aguish calenture—but an improvement nonetheless—even as Farounwi sustained the towelling of his body, especially his temple and head, down to his long cold legs.

But The Nomad's soul had gradually slunk out of his bones onto ether, his very scenery had become an immaculate cloudscape of sheer jouissance: Like palm cockatoos, two gaily figures are seen playing the wood block and cowbell with glistening mallets, joined in view by an accompanying set playing the piano, an accordion, and some strings, all trailed in view by another set of the band consisting of a figure playing the variable-pitch drum, Omele, with infectious attention and other percussionists beating the drum kit and the prosodic Bàtá, Sákárà and Gangan. They are joined in play by coroneted chorines and baritonal voices, altogether donning lucent capes and making high-spirited sounds from an open-roof caravanette like an Elysian callithump. Their unalloyed delight is palpable, and The Nomad's phantasmagoria appeared rooted in reality, which he was also beginning to relish.

Yet, The Nomad could sense the transitoriness of this reality, its fleeting non-static nature, like flickers of sunburst; appearing, disappearing and reappearing like shades of penumbral floodlight, roving over a vast unwinding declivity of this now and that later. More than anything, he could feel himself fighting a certain paralysis, a respiratory contraction, a chilling fluctuation between soteriology and eschatology, a mysterious force whose disenable intent seemed to alert him to his powerlessness; a determinist gust illuding him to yield to intractable surrealism, a world so desired and yet so submerged in menacing antinomies. He tried to efface himself from it all, from his complexly woven psychosomatic froth, to escape the watchful eyes of wrynecks surveilling his brittle, even manic expressions like monitor lizards; the paradoxical taxidermy of floating widgeons and sedentary black grouse on a coppiced shrub; a herd of mastodons and mammoths marching by the gross as if towards him with overlong tusks and prehensile trunks.

But just as quickly he was therewith plunged into a different realm of accretive alterations: a process of unfurling that emerged as an interminable mist, throwing up behind its misty veil a lanky hatchet-faced masculine creature, unsmiling and dewhiskered and sartorially covered in embroidered grey-oak Babariga and nut-brown kufi hat. He was seated behind a modish bureau desk spotting a dainty tabletop printer, well-reclined with his hands perfectly fixed to his ergonomic armchair, his veiny skull sticking out across his pretentious facial expression. And on the other side of the bureau was The Nomad, unmistakably recognizable in his metempsychotic form—upright and neatly clothed in a single vent slim-fit suit, tailored drainpipe trousers and a pratt-knot tie.

'Lanre Atiba, sir...'

'You may sit,' said the metempsychotic Hassan, who immediately continued:

'I have looked at your résumé and decided to offer you a job as my—'

A sudden noise replete with agonizing screams of tragicomic voices, accompanied by a frenzied blast of wind, increasingly deafened The Nomad to the rest of whatever he could sense Hassan saying. He was perceptive enough to feel himself absorbing the disagreeably bedizened room in which he stood: the bureau desk was still noticeable, the heraldic frames blazoned across his distended vision and other varied forms of obscurities hugging the walls seemed like a shadowy hypostatization of some hellish microcosm, the voice of his potential employer, Hassan, sounded more like the voice of a cruel tormentor than an innocuous converser. All about him, he could sense himself losing control, like his brain was going through a process of intractable noetic siltation—admitting all kinds of grotesque matter determined to render his vision torturous. At once, he could sense his whole being undergoing a diffusion towards a synapse where unsolicited creatures and tiny gnats are perceptibly billowing out of the pollution taking over his faculties, marching threateningly about him, seemingly determined to rend him into mangled shards for their exogenous extravagancies. Indeed, he began wondering if these elements polluting his vision were some form of reincarnation of actual existence or reality.

'Am I witnessing a desperate instance of material extinction?' The Nomad asked inaudibly and unconsciously.

As this question pullulated by degrees all over his mind, his capacity to restrain his paranoia, especially with what seemed the wicked obstinacy of his unmoved assailants, gradually eroded into oblivion. In a tick, The Nomad's execration of his perceived assailants began swirling around his cloaca, his desire being nothing but to cause them all to be swallowed in a fitting scatologic sump. Yet he could not rein in the overwhelming urge to mutter prayers to any halocline phenomena that would heed his supplications and sunder him from his delirious torture. But the tone of his prayers would change as he, again, began staggering towards the dreaded synapse that foreshadowed his existential finality and capitulation to nullity.

The Nomad's approach towards this vague synapse seemed to have been accompanied by an extraordinary somatic tremor, such that Baba Faleke—who, alongside Fagbami, had several minutes earlier joined Farounwi in observing The Nomad in the material world—bade Fagbami to quickly make a sugared sanative potion for The Nomad.

'Ori ti o royin ogun ni, ko ni ku si oju ogun; akuko ti o ko laba ni, asa o gbodo gbe loro modiye[4],' averred Baba Faleke for the first time since he installed himself in the slipper chair by the casement, watching The Nomad like a sessile barnacle, his visage brimming with reassurance, a true sacerdotal reassurance. Now reminded of something he should have instructed Fagbami to include in the sugared purée, he promptly got up from his chair and made for the skillion where Fagbami was preparing the elixir.

But The Nomad, though barely conscious, had a different perception of the goings-on in the material world. The movements about him were inextricably infused into his delirious Gehenna so that as Baba Faleke and Fagbami made for the skillion, their one-time movement became a series of tearing replications, repeating itself over and over like thunderous crepitations—at one time appearing as a herd of flying flamingos, porcupines, ibexes and wild boars accompanied by passional paparazzi capturing their sally in real-time, and at other times appearing as a thousand different unnameable and menacing creatures.

Everything was real and unreal at the same time; rationality and irrationality became asymmetric renditions of the same grotesque matter. Yet he could feel his feet doddering towards this unknown grotesquerie. The clock on the office wall from which he perceived his deliriant psychoacoustics, however illusive, became an ominous carrier of transcendent impulses; the last ramparts of his material existence, as he felt it, were beginning to crumble and there was nothing he could do to stop it. Every plock that emerged from the clock left a reverberant bong note in his entrails that seemed to herald the ticking away

---

4   He that will describe the ravages of war shall survive its course; a cock that will crow at
     courtyard must never be preyed on by the hawk-eagle.

of his very being—like a celestial knell presaging the arrival of irreversible finality. Every passing minute sent him closer to his end: he could see it, feel it, but could neither reverse it nor appeal for clemency.

In an instant he felt himself dropping into a cathartic yet despondent morass, greeting helplessly so that he even began to regard himself as some degenerate who was deserving of nothing but damnation. He felt the urge to writhe in the gunk of soteriological confession—sensing and suspecting his own senses at the same time—that it might save him from his imminent evaporation. As each clock-tick shuffled him towards the dreaded synapse, he started to feel his heartbeat plunging for its nadir like a drowning frogman, accompanied by what seemed the caws of carrion crows, and unconsciously, he began to reel off a persistent swan song:

Here comes the last hour,
I am about to meet my maker,
The last hour is now!
The last hour is now!
The last hour is now!

But Baba Faleke and Fagbami had returned to the room accompanied by a flustered belle whose glowing molasses-like skin would under normal circumstances have whetted The Nomad's affectionate appetite. The Nomad's lament, at this point, had become quaveringly sonorous that it seemed a firm repudiation of agonistic impulses. In his delirium, he could feel the thorny sting of his wistful longing for salvation—a contradiction of his desperate desire in the material world to, by any means, breathe his last. Baba Faleke, grasping his Iroke Ifá or Divination Tapper in one hand, began chanting a mythological incantation.

'Serve it to him now,' Baba Faleke bade Farounwi immediately after.

But every attempt made by Farounwi and later Fagbami went down the tubes, and neither did Baba Faleke himself succeed in making The Nomad drink the elixir, leaving him clucking confusingly. To The Nomad, the three men were dreadful agonistic creatures rehearsing his funeral oration. And so he inflexibly rejected the elixir, perceiving it as nothing but envenomed toxin.

Tilting his head upwards like a supplicant to Olodumare on The Nomad's behalf, Baba Faleke mumbled what seemed the supplication of the suppliant Danaus:

'but if fortune smile, if death be driven away,

Vowed rites, with eager haste, we to the gods will pay!'

—'Let me try,' said Iwa, the belle in the room, as she leapt towards Baba Faleke to take over the onerous task.

Apparelled in a floaty paprika robe worn over a salmon-pink camisole covering her pneumatic bust, Iwa had been brought up to speed on The Nomad's condition when she joined her father and the acolytes at the skillion. Now, with her head slightly inclined forward, she approached The Nomad in a gentle solicitous manner.

'Hello,' she said; 'I am here with my father to help you get well. We are trying to help you, not harm you; if you don't take this elixir, it may be too difficult for us to help. Do you understand?'

The Nomad gave no response.

'Please, take this,' said Iwa.

Haltingly, The Nomad, squinty-eyed and blank, looked vaguely into her eyes, questioning and unquestioning himself on his familiarity with her vague countenance and the thought that she meant no harm; for she was at that moment neither fish nor fowl nor good red herring. The vagueness of her form rendered his capacity for discernment even more involved, and before long he began flailing about in a warren of crashing sub-realities. His addled perception of Iwa had suddenly undergone a metastasis in which Iwa's form had become the figure of a tormentor, on the other side of barbed iron grilles erected to pigeonhole him to a catacomb of non-existential fantasies; her very sight had become an ogrish personification, circumscribed by a smorgasbord of fiendish creatures, all determined to ensure he remained cooped up in their brutish world—once he sipped the damned toxin. Even if he wouldn't survive this turmoil, he thought, he must deny this gorgon every jot of *schadenfreude* she desired.

Then, suddenly, he peered into the gourd bowl in Iwa's hands and instead of the potable elixir, or the liquid slopped over the edges of the gourd, his deliriant eyes only saw a bullring in which he was the non-matador bait for menacing bulls and also the fascination of morbid spectators goading him towards the querencia. Unmediated, he descended into a trance-like realm in which all he had ever hoped to become in life pelted down on him like a ton of bricks, then stuck to his vision a little while more until he could no longer bear the lances of elusive yearnings. He flinched backwards at once, waving his head as though more unwilling to take the potion now than somewhat, and mumbled on and on indistinctly.

Determined to serve The Nomad the sanative mixture, Iwa handed the gourd bowl to Fagbami, motioned him and her father to take a few steps back while she stretched out both hands and held The Nomad's face, muttering words to him almost in strict confidence. 'It's for your recovery, don't think otherwise,' Iwa said, repeating her adjuration again and again in an attempt to disrupt his fantastical mumbling. Then, gradually, she got him to slightly part his lips, quickly recovered the gourd bowl from Fagbami and served the potable elixir to The Nomad.

In a tick, a ripple of noticeable relief darted through the ambience of the room, just as a burst of juddery sensations surged through The Nomad's spine and goose pimples spread through his hair follicles. As he became less deliriant, his vision became a tad more promising. His eyes stubbornly wanting to bear witness, all he could make of the moving lips of Baba Faleke and his allies, was a Steinlauf-seeming recitation alerting him to the attainableness of his survival, asking him to direct his *cri-de-coeur* for life to Èsù, the arbiter of the crossroads between life and death, bidding him to pull himself from his delirious barracoon.

PART 3

Cry for the broken tribe, for the law and the custom that is gone. Aye, and cry aloud for the man who is dead, for the woman and children bereaved. Cry, the beloved country, these things are not yet at an end. The sun pours down on the earth, on the lovely land that man cannot enjoy. He knows only the fear of his heart.

—Alan Paton
Cry, the Beloved Country

I t was a noiseless, cheery and fitting morning to be up with the lark in Southern Audoghast. The fleeting whistles of the wind were soused in the uneasy calm that the day itself embodied, and the overarching spirit of the day, tangible and gripping, shot through the veins like a gust of benign energy, enkindling as the ground which effused a kindred unexplainable quality. The same ground was on this day a conduit for ferrying The Nomad's rebellious feeling, alongside his friend and other dissenters, towards the atrocious institution chipping away at the dignity of young Southern Audoghastans.

As shafts of light began to break through the veil blanketing the face of dawn, a tenacious stirring began to coagulate in marching clusters, mutating in strength with every crook, ascent, tilt and slant of the road, increasingly peopled by demonstrators from all corners and recesses of Southern Audoghast. A civilian outpouring of evocative effusions, seething with rebellious ebullition, each one inspired by a passionate vim rooted in justice, resolved to confront the double-pronged force of state and non-state aggression; the one acting with vicious arbitrariness like a possessed mannequin, the other acting under the grip of savage stimuli. A few miles to the main assemblage, the partly-tarred route was covered with footmarks of all kinds, stretching as the crow flies on all sides. It was hardly believable that just the previous day, the same road had been almost unpeopled—tranquil and merely dotted here and there with bullocking entities.

And yet there had been a permanently scarring maelstrom on that day, engineered by the indigent ciphers for nefarious intrigues, hired from the bowels of societal rejection and social mis-conditioning, to scuttle the peaceable fulminations of ill-treated citizens against the habitual abuse of power by a murderous Gestapo masquerading as a disciplined police unit defending the common weal. A decadent branch evidences a cancerous root, which must be uprooted and burnt to cinders—argued the protesters. But while their argument resonated not with the deep state steering the direction of public policy, it struck an irrepressible chord in The Nomad's entrails, just as it did with multitudes of people in Southern Audoghast. In fine, a protest against police brutality, otherwise moderate and virtually unavailing, had been recklessly propelled by the state and its socially vulnerable ciphers to excite the indignant psyche of the Southern Audoghast collective. On that day, the state-backed aggression of violent marionettes against the peaceful pickets of the Audoghast Police Force Headquarters demanding justice, as well as the heartless vandalization of the protesters' private properties at the picket ground by the hired ruffians, provoked a groundswell of unprecedented public indignation. This indignation inflamed an instant impulse of solidarity in The Nomad.

Later that night, a bold television reportage detailed what had happened earlier in the day: 'The Special Anti-Crime Unit of the Audoghast Police Force killed my brother last week; he only went out to pick up his fast-food before he was fatally shot. My heart is charged with anger, and my soul is wracked with sorrow because the police have refused to punish the guilty officer, even though his identity is publicly known,' said Ifeoma George—a five-foot, thickset, light-coloured, twenty-something lady—speaking from the bowered shade of an alley wherein she had taken shelter with a handful of others avoiding the combined bestiality of hired ruffians and police water cannons and teargas canisters—'but you can see what they have done to me,' she continued, nudging the cameraman to capture the gash in her bloodied ankle.

'Rather than explain why my law-abiding brother was shot to death by the Special Anti-Crime Unit of the Force, they responded by firing multiple tear gas canisters at us until my leg became like this,' she concluded, waving her head lamentably, her bloodstained eyes screaming rage and mournfulness at the same time.

'Those bastards! May psoriasis—nay, amoebic dysentery—plague them for the rest of their lives! We will be back tomorrow!' said a conspicuously galled protester standing abreast of Ifeoma.

'All docility have limits,' said The Nomad, as he instantly rang his three friends jointly and informed them of his intention to partake in the next day's protest against police brutality. In the same breath, he texted his principal at work:

'Dear Hassan, I am sorry to inform you that I will be absent from the office tomorrow. I apologize for every inconvenience this might cause, but I promise to resume next week.'

The following morning, Ìgè showed up at The Nomad's abode to drive him to the protest while Ajégbèmí and Lánléhìn made their way to work. As they drove towards the protest ground, The Nomad pulled his mobile from his pocket and read his texts with Hassan again, seething with sheer frustration:

'We are meeting someone important tomorrow, as you know, and I want you at the office.' replied Hassan.

'My apologies, Hassan, but I can't make it to the office. I thought I was ready to resume after what happened… but I am not.'

'Consider yourself cashiered if you don't show up tomorrow,' Hassan responded brusquely.

A resultant rash of inquietude flitted through The Nomad's soul case, and he jerked his head as if to banish his restlessness to Hades. At that moment, something about the exchange rankled him, inch by inch, like patches of unwanted papules. He sniggered at the thought, at the olid guts which Hassan's message reeked of the day before. *Cashiered*, he mumbled in his mind, as he sniggered again, bristling with disbelief, slighted by the sheer nerve of the word—of Hassan's temerity to even think of that word, let alone type it up and send to him. He wondered if the filthy bastard would have dared say it to his face: *he sure would never have*, The Nomad fancied himself. In reality, though, he knew he would have done nothing; he would have been unable to do anything, not a groat of anything tangible in that putrescent Audoghast. At most, he thought, he would have been thrown out of countenance by the sheer audacity which such a venture—to have him cashiered—would have demanded, and it probably would have been hard to stomach—or not. But, ultimately, he thought, he would have had to clamber out of that grinding blight, which would have formed not only from the fact of losing his job 'dishonourably' but also the fact of losing it despite what he could have done—what he could have summoned from his overcharged armoury to secure his position. Even so, he saw that scandalous experience to be less an armoury and more a cumbersome burden. *Oh, what a spineless fool I must be!* The Nomad laced into himself.

Then he looked out of the window to the heavy sky and suddenly remembered the day he came to abominate Hassan; what he had witnessed on that day, he recalled, was the terminal nail in the coffin of Hassan's constant flirt with the abominable. There had been instances of what The Nomad regarded as condonable absurdities before, but none was ever as monstrously absurd as what he had seen with his two eyes on that day. He had, after all, stomached the repulsive incident at The Bassianus Hotel, where he had chanced on Senator Jibril, a notorious, bandy-legged Northern Audoghast politician, buggering Hassan. He had crept towards Hassan's room that night after initially checking out the other three rooms in that presidential suite, unsure if the husky and grainy whimpers reaching his ears were those of a flattening player piano that had somehow installed itself in that commodious space. But the spyhole had sufficiently exploded his doubts.

And how he had wished to creep out of the suite unnoticed but failed, in the end, when his ponderous feet, considerably strained and reeling in a daze, crashed into bottles of beer clustered on the marble flooring until they ricocheted in block-spoked boomerang. Days and countless hours of frigid and nervous interplay had followed between The Nomad and Hassan until, some day, it became a condonable absurdity for him to see Hassan and Jibril in their rompy element, as if those frosty days and hours had dissolved into a sort of mandatory toleration. Perhaps it became tolerable, albeit relatively, when Hassan hesitantly related to The Nomad that his frequent buggery with political big weights was part of a series of 'calculated commitments', to win lucrative white elephant projects from the Federal Government. Yet, the fact that Hassan was a calculated homosexual did little to prevail on The Nomad: from time to time, The Nomad would brood over the fact that Hassan Umaru, a 27-year-old Political Consultant from Northern Audoghast, who was three years his junior, would so desperately disdain the notion of 'riches without wings,' and would rather be a greed-sodden, cringe-making social climber, offering his dookiehole to men the age of his grandfather.

But even the pretext of being a calculated homosexual, despite having several heterosexual flings on the side, was insufficient to assuage The Nomad's spleen nor tame his feral disgust at his sighting of this particular horror, which he thought was simply the nadir of obscenities. It had happened barely a week before that momentous day of the demonstration. Hassan had returned from lunch with Mina, one of his other regular flings, and had repaired to the sanctum of his office, as they often did together. But an emergency message from one of Hassan's political benefactors, which The Nomad had received as Hassan's personal assistant while the latter was most likely on the job and unable to attend to his phone, had forced The Nomad to invade Hassan's sanctum. Such emergencies sometimes proved advantageous to the firm. But no sooner had The Nomad breezed into Hassan's office than his sensorial organs got assailed by both the filming tripod at the centre of Hassan's office and the stench of excreta which pervaded the room. By the time The Nomad cocked his head in the direction of the nook which led to the comfort room, all he could see was a passageway leading to the scatologic sacrarium of Elagabalus. Hassan, in the raw and in a crouched posture, was sensually funnelling his excrement into the mouth of Mina, who was spreadeagled and in the nude with hands imbrued with faecal filth, cheerfully play-acting the role of a damned coprophiliac. Staggered and petrified to the utmost degree, The Nomad remained fixed to the same spot until he suddenly found the strength to scurry out of Hassan's office, long before the stunned scuzzball had been able to gather his wits.

At this point, The Nomad's features had transmogrified into wrinkles of emetic expressions, as though he were doubly reliving the horrors all over again. Somehow, he had come to regard that insufferable moment as a monumental one, often repeating to himself in his brown study—tinged, nonetheless, with croaks of derisive bewilderment—that there was a depth, a clod of mysteries about that moment that he was yet to plumb. The entire affair could have played out differently: Hassan and Mina could have securely shut the door to that office, or they could have concealed themselves in the roomy comfort room, not to mention they could have booked a hotel or gone to Hassan's residence. Of all places, the office was the one rendezvous such sight of wretched obscenity should have neither been brooked nor ventured. Yet it was the exact place they had chosen to exalt the cult of Elagabalus, Hassan himself transformed into a Sardanapalus redivivus. There was no doubt in The Nomad's mind that this was not just against the stream; it was the very extremity of cosmic asininity, of even those condonable absurdities he had entertained as venial excrescences unrelated to Hassan's underlying humanity. Now, he found himself regarding even that calculated homosexual underside of Hassan as much preferred, much excusable than this extraterrestrial affliction whitewashed as some newfangled kink, some pardonable insanity, some degenerate pedestal of civilization from which even prehistoric creatures must have fled like the bubonic plague. *How the twenty-first century has become the dungheap of humanity's worst inclinations! How the so-called rising generation has become the embodiment of cosmic decadence!*—he exclaimed in his mind.

Since that experience, he had utterly avoided the office and not by a long shot thought of returning to that abyss of perdition, except for the planned meeting on the day of the protest. At the time, he was still unsure whether to resign or retain his position. His precarious middle-classness relied heavily on what he earned at Hassan's firm. And despite this dilemma, his disgusted mind was brimming with a certain sense of sureness— one that stemmed from an unasked but expected allegiance— that conscience-stricken allegiance he had expected of Hassan. Thus, it was exasperating reading he could lose his job: the same job, he thought, which he had done so far with such fidelity so rare and costly in the whole of Audoghast. The job was, after all, not only the bulwark that shielded him from losing his sanity, that kept him afloat in an entropic economy, but also the wedge which prevented him from caving in to the unshaped weight of disgust. It was this job, with all its strangling discomfitures, that had somehow helped him in locating Hemeroscopium—that formless place into which he had banished everything rebellious and sententious in his inherent nature.

He knew it was a risk too unthinkable, a venture too moronic, to attempt blowing the whistle on even that corrosive buggery pathology that Hassan was afflicted with, much less the scatologic obscenity. He knew too well that, in the main, those who legislated against such obscenities in Audoghast were at the same time their foremost indulgers, treacherously and invariably in cahoots with law enforcers.

'Are you okay?' asked Ìgè, unwittingly recalling The Nomad to his immediate environment.

'Absolutely,' The Nomad responded firmly, determined to go the whole hog and join the protest. Inwardly, he desired nepenthe, if he could have it.

'Let's park there,' he said to Ìgè, waving to a parking garage nearby.

As they started for the barricades, The Nomad was enchanted with the impassioned boutades of other dissenters: 'we have the right to live!' hollered the one, 'we will never be intimidated!' bellowed the other. Each dissenter had a unique manner of expression, even gesticulation, which ignited rebellious flames in the rest. They moved with such vehemence that may be likened to the ardour of those glorious stormers of the Bastille, and yet they collectively exuded a sense of composure that dispelled any hint of extremity. Nonetheless, calm and passion are mummified antagonists, ever condemned to combustible eruption.

The assemblage, which amassed several hundreds of people, was animated by various side activities which initially left The Nomad at sea as to the real purpose of the gathering, especially after seeing some would-be glitterati getting crunk on Afrobeats and hip-hop. But these side activities—from the gospelizing zealots on one extreme end to the self-absorbed clusters pottering around, sloganeering and interacting sotto voce with one another, and the vendors sorting edibles and designing handwritten placards in their shaded corner—by and by gave way to the vibrant feminine voice that collected all protesters into a compact aggregate for demonstration.

The Nomad and Ìgè found themselves at the frontline of the demonstration, iterating harmonized responses to specific protest slogans. Impassioned speakers took turns to condemn what was collectively perceived as a case of systemic viciousness, gross abuse of human rights and unchecked impunity by that unit of the Force. And soon, the megaphone was randomly passed to The Nomad, whose hortatory rendition went thus:

'Great Southern Audoghast!'

'Great!' the assemblage responded.

'Great Southern Audoghast!'

'Great!'

'Great Southern Audoghast!'

Great!'

'I am here today' said The Nomad, 'because I now understand, like you all, that we have failed to call those whom we like to regard as friends by their true name. We have taken for friends wild hyenas and failed to discern the claws of savage tigers. Look around you, and you will see that all of us—men and women, parents and children, friends and rivals, swains and trysters—are expendable pieces in the sadistic game of our police friends. Our friends in the Audoghast Police Force (indeed we are incessantly reminded that they are our friends) have stabbed us more times than a bushel of thorns would ever have pricked our skin. These Brutus-like friends of ours have brutally and continuously dispatched our brothers and sisters like some footling game in the wild. By camouflaging as our friends, the good men and women who wear the blood-soaked uniform of the Audoghast Police Force have killed those we love unremittingly and without remorse and constituted themselves as our real tormentors. Yet they say they are our friends and demand that we approach them with benign aspects. These friends of ours, whose smiles never fail to precipitate our tears, whose truncheons never fail to bludgeon our heads, whose breaths never fail to foretell our deaths, whose guns never cease to precipitate our caskets, are so good a friend to us that our friendship with them can only mean the naïve embrace of our own end. These fiends that we call friends, will only be our friends as long as we allow them to hogtie us to the treacherous pendulum of life at their command.

'Remember our Southern Audoghast sister, Ifeoma George, who, yesterday, came to our self-proclaimed friends—the Audoghast Police Force—to demand justice for the vicious elimination of her only brother by the uncircumcised venoms in their ranks? What did these good friends of ours do? They drove her and the other pickets off like pesky flies—and inflicted injuries on them to boot. And, let's not forget: they also hired street villains to complement their 'friendly' onslaught! My fellow compatriots, if no one else will tell us the truth, let our tongues be not too reluctant to find expression. A man with many friends is an enemy of himself. And so I ask: for how long?'

'No more!' howled the assemblage.

'I say, my fellow Southern Audoghastans, for how long shall we continue to call friends those who move as fiends against us?'

'No more!'

'In that case,' continued The Nomad, 'we must demand justice, for Emmanuel George, Ifeoma's brother; for Adeolu, the young man who was bumped off before Emmanuel; and for the countless others whose names inflict unmitigated agonies on our consciences. We must demand the abolishment of that rogue unit of the Audoghast Police Force, and demand to be treated not as friends but as humans.'

'No more! No more!!' bellowed the assemblage, as Ajégbèmí and Lánléhìn—both convinced that The Nomad was on the wrong tram and duly told him during their conversation the previous night, but decided to take advantage of their lunch break to briefly join the demonstrators nonetheless—wended their way to the frontline where The Nomad was airing his inflaming declamations.

'Isn't it astonishing?' Lánléhìn queried Ajégbèmí under his breath, as they immersed themselves in the passionate eruptions spreading through the atmosphere, looking about and listening to The Nomad who had a complete grip over his audience.

'It really is,' Ajégbèmí blurted out in response, 'it's as if he's been planning to do this for ages.'

'Looks like we just might have a chance, you know,' said Lánléhìn, referring to the contrast between what was playing out on the protest ground and the crux of the opposing opinion during their four-way call the previous night. Ajégbèmí had argued against participating in the demonstration, maintaining that nobody wins against the state.

Now, in response, he simply shrugged as though to say 'we shall see.'

—'But,' resumed again The Nomad, 'we underserve ourselves if we remain assembled here, several miles away from where our so-called friends are deployed to our homes and neighbourhoods to slaughter us.'

'Now then, where shall we go?' asked one of the demonstrators.

'To their command post here in Southern Audoghast!' retorted The Nomad.

'You ask us to return to the lion's den despite yesterday's narrow escape?' said another demonstrator.

'Yes. Our lives are not any more endangered here than they would be there. If any of us here today is too timid to face up to death, then our gathering is pointless.'

'To their command post!' an enkindled demonstrator piped up.

'To their command post!' chorused some other demonstrators.

'Caution,' warned The Nomad, 'our march to the command post should be guided not by the fierceness of our emotions but by the justness of our cause. The appropriateness of our aim should undergird our actions. The song of abolishment and reform should vitalize our feet and dissuade us from all extremities.'

'Yes!' exclaimed some demonstrators.

'No violence! We just want to be heard!' avowed Lánléhìn from his frontline position beside Ajégbèmí, as other demonstrators took up the chant 'no violence, we just want to be heard!' and repeated it over and over.

And just at that moment, two currant red coaches drew up behind the assemblage and disgorged shabbily-clothed armed ruffians, one-half of their faces masked with cookie-cutter bandanas, their upper arms wrapped with amulets and in all respects looking like they had been caked in sludge before storming the protest ground. About a dozen of them took the prow brandishing broad-rimmed locally made machetes, their hands bandaged with off-white leathery fabrics that glued the weapon's base to the pads of their street-hardened palms, grippy and more than ready to strike. Behind them, files of explosive heavy-jowled roughnecks spiralled out in menacing formation, discoloured wooden bats, biggish sticks of various lengths, and sharp-toothed handsaws punching the possessive air that forged an ugly rush above their heads. In the next breath, they began yammering in kabbalistic tongues as their bloodthirsty hands aviated the course of their destruction. In a flash, they charged at the shell-shocked assemblage as though the floodgates of fanatic carnage had at long last been thrown open, taking full advantage of the real sense that the demonstrators had been caught on the hop. At once, the whole place was down to the ground engulfed by a violent maelstrom, as the protesters scampered in every direction away from their aggressors, whose ferity intensified alongside their violent fanatic chants.

Terry, a stumpy, round-shouldered protester, had fallen prey to the ruffians, his face horribly mutilated with machetes and reduced to a mass of pulp. Deborah, a short and stout protester, had suffered a hiding so thorough no one was in doubt they had thrashed the living daylights out of her. Several cars, speaker systems and various appurtenances had suffered unspeakable vandalization.

The larger chunk of the protesters, along with The Nomad, who had scampered off in the first instance were suddenly stopped on the fly as The Nomad decided on the spot to put his finger in the dyke.

'Now now,' The Nomad called out, 'where in tarnation are we scampering to! We must either confront those *slubberdegullions* now or we will never be able to nail our colours to the mast!'

In turn, a masculine, astringent voice bellowed at once, 'put them to rout!'

The response of the protesters, male and female, was swift and momentous. At once, they surged like a firestorm at the ruffians and were before long fully embroiled in an all-out brawl. Rankled to the nth degree by the savage brashness of their aggressors, it only took a while before the demonstrators outfaced the ruffians. Four unfortunate atomies among the hired roughnecks were collared and properly whacked, suffering lacerations to the temple and shanks so that the beatings were intermitted only when they were patently more dead than alive and in a short time despatched to the nearest hospital.

At the same time, plumes of dark cumuli gathered ominously in the lour sky, roving as wisps of detached cloudlets sown with gloomy vapours, even though the ruck of the protesters was still overborne by sheer incredulity and the fact that they had made mincemeat of unexampled savage aggressors.

Waddling through the ruck, however, was Ajégbèmí, trailed by Ige and three visibly dispirited pallbearers conveying a stopgap bier in which there laid a motionless Lánléhìn, unconscious and bloodied from head to toe, his metallic-blue jacket dripping gore and wrapped around the gash in his forehead. Witnessing this, The Nomad was instantly rooted to the ground like a deer in the headlights and remained shell-shocked to the core. But an irate Ajégbèmí would not have it.

'This... is because of you. This… is your fault! This is your corpse and you must carry it!' Ajégbèmí exclaimed, scowling at The Nomad dolefully.

Armed to the teeth, three Audoghast Police officers interrupted the subdued scene out of the blue, essaying to arrest The Nomad and two others.

'For what!' roared a protester among the ruck, all of whose hackles had begun to rise.

'For questioning,' replied one officer.

'Moonshine! Questioning for what?' volleyed another protester.

'Go and ask your father!' a square-faced officer snapped at him, just as a handful of protesters countered with dramatic fulmination.

'Where were you just now when those accursed hoodlums violently disrupted our peaceful demonstration?' asked a female protester, croaking with disbelief.

'They were diverting themselves from the sidelines in that corner,' said another protester pointing to the jalopy truck only a few yards from the protest ground.

Then, with a scowl on his face and like a bull at a gate, one incensed, buff and neckbearded protester named Lanko emerged from the ruck, removed his silver-rimmed shades, and discharged his wrath with such ferocious outburst:

'I swear on the graves of my grandmother, my grandfather, my father and my mother: not a single protester will leave here with any of you. Never a one!'

'Okay boys, you heard him. Lump it and march on now!' barracked another protester, as the others joined her in rapid succession.

The brewing bedlam was shaping up to be a terrible bummer for the officers; they could sense a frightful omen in the air: Something about Lanko's outburst and the changing mood of the protesters had caused the officers' misguided ardour to wane, especially considering their cat's paws had also been outfaced. By and by, they shuffled their clumpy boots and beat a retreat, causing their half-witted intrigue to come to nothing.

Immediately, a suppressed relish flitted through the atmosphere, and Lanko earned an all-round pat on the back, except from The Nomad who was still fixed to the ground like a stunned mullet. Beyond him, Ìgè and a covey of willing protesters took up the task of transporting Lánléhìn's remains to the morgue, completely excluding The Nomad from the process due to his manifest agony and deep-rooted necrophobia, which Ige had discovered during the burial of Mama Jebba. But far from being out of the woods, the demonstrators were only hopping from skillet to kiln as a file of Saracen tanks and police trucks blaring sirens soon drew up in view. Seeing this, the protesters brooked little doubt that the fearsome cavalcade foretold a grim omen.

Indeed, making no attempts to dispel the unease of the demonstrators, the trucks poured out a horde of warlike and formidably armed troops who, without any warning, launched a bestial mass slaughter of the defenceless protesters. In a flash, the scene dissolved into chaos as the protesters scampered in all directions like heedless chickens. The Nomad was at once jolted back to consciousness and scurried to cover unhurt; and so did Ajégbèmí and several other protesters. In a matter of minutes, the scene was thickly covered with wounded and lifeless bodies.

Lying prostrate from a shared coverture, Ajégbèmí jerked his head all of a sudden, shot daggers at The Nomad for a moment, then sped off like a bat out of hell to the decimation hotspot.

He never returned.

PART 4

*A man was born to die continually
and start afresh.*

—Ngũgĩ Wa Thiong'o
A Grain of Wheat

8

A dreamy vista unfurled itself to The Nomad as he stared fixedly at a youngster picking his teeth in a static posture on an uncrowded footway, flanked sinistrally by waspish hucksters, grifters and the likes, and dextrally by cosy tattlers chewing the rag. Following in view was a pageant of rufescent barges answering to the dexterous steering of bargemen coursing through a rambling sodalite watercourse, and above this line were roundels of oil sketches and intaglioed pyxides displaying half-vague, half-lucid images. The backwaters cropped up in view, dotted with three-legged ostriches, jerboas and kangaroos, all hopping about like a dog with two tails. Gradually, this view began to recede as if tethered to a grapnel pulling it against its will, evanescing by and by into the nebulous shades of nothingness until a terra firma cropped up rudely in full view. Just as quickly, a heavy-duty open-top truck the size of a gigantic ocean shot menacingly towards The Nomad, only to again vanish like a streak, as if blown out by a gale.

Slowly, he found before his eyes an escarpment overlooking browny mudflats caving in to the exertions of an unseen force which, before long, caused his view to puff out to a roomy sanctum where The Nomad could see his teenage self, lying sidewards and facing a beanpole chap of similar age. Both teenagers giggled and leered at each other so carnally that, in no time, they were cuddled up in each other's arms; the one intermittently jerking his head and leaning towards the other who lent his lips amorously until both had their lips affectionately entwined. In a short time, the teenage Nomad laid spreadeagled as the other chap began to play his hands across his carnal form, trailing one finger by the other until all his fingers in full swing glided down the teenage Nomad's underpants.

Suddenly, they were jolted out of character by the footfalls of an approaching blurry figure who, in full view, proved to be a squab canon in soutane and tasselled fascia and whose unsuspecting purpose at that moment seemed to have been to bid the teenagers to hit the sack. As the canon turned his back to leave, both teenagers speedily genuflected penitently as though to adjure him to relieve them of the guilt of verboten self-indulgence, to which he agreed like a shot.

Almost in the same breath, a heated dispute breaks out in view in a completely different *mise-en-scène* in which a grotty nightclub with a simple design, bulging at the seams with vampy women of the streets in the state of dishabille, one of which The Nomad—tottering like one who had had one over the eight—had fancied to the hilt. It was behind closed doors where, no sooner had The Nomad cupped her globes and ventured to do the other than a gang of truculent hotheads stopped him in the act, the ringleader in high dudgeon and visibly spoiling for a fight.

'You dunce, she belongs to me!' said the ringleader, a stern-looking, rock-faced, diminutive mesomorph.

'Oh caramba! But she is just a slut,' The Nomad piped up.

But there and then, a wrathful deluge of disorienting smacks and sidewinders bombarded his face—time and again—until he started to feel lumps of flesh coming off his facial tissue, so that instantly he began to understand the reverberations of his unguarded return. But it was too late to undo his wrong. His attempts to sue for leniency, first from the gang in general and later from a specific gang member with a familiar profile, went down the gurgler.

'Boss, dem don unstream me[5],' said the speculative acquaintance whose sole mode of recognition to The Nomad was his tenebrous countenance.

In a wink, The Nomad was carried off by the gang into a pitch-dark grotto.

• • • •

The moon was now in her full complement, her very irradiance bulging through the uncurtained casement with pronounced glints of hopefulness. Countless stars spread out in sidereal constellations like bunting in the sky, and Iwa, donning a rose-coloured peekaboo blouse and having spent long hours darning in a poshly padded armchair about three yards from the bedstead, had drifted off to the trills of songbirds. Two days had passed since The Nomad went out like a light, though Iwa had been wet-nursing him ever since. Her housebroken cat, Trisha, switching beats between The Nomad's place on the bed and being glommed on to Iwa's heels, pottered about and purred mushily.

---

5   Brother, I wield no power here.

From a stone's throw outside, on one of the planter benches, Fagbami and Farounwi are winding down their drawn-out tête-à-tête.

'I bet if we weren't here to witness all Iwa is doing for this man,' said Farounwi, 'we would easily brand anyone telling us of her tender care for the stranger a soothsayer of sorts.'

'Exactly. But, why do you think this is happening at all?' asked Fagbami. 'There are enough hands here to help the stranger if only she would allow it.'

'Not to make a mountain out of a molehill,' said Farounwi, halting his response to look around for a second, 'but I think she is making a dead set at him.'

'Ah! What if he wakes up and isn't taken to her?'

'Well, let's hope that her plans—if, indeed, she has them—do not go down the tubes.'

'May Ifá, the knower of all hearts and wishes, guide her path,' Fagbami concluded.

• • • •

The swishy sound of a diamantine hourglass erupts sonorously from a sedate sylvan vista accompanied by an emerging high-octane, elephantine drivetrain, spinning with kinetic discipline and propelling a ceiba-like seven-vaned turbine as if towards the hourglass. By some means, this peculiar field of vision pales by comparison in torturous ramifications to the reverberative tick-tocks of a giant device emerging in sight, at first hazily half-balanced on an unseen structure, but eventually crystallizing as a pendent metronome asymptotically unreeving itself from a drawn-out high-wire, hued like a cattle egret and emerging

142

louder as it inched closer through a pintle hitch with rumbling loudness, sentiently threatening an acoustic shock.

In an instant, The Nomad's sight was transposed to an embodiment of himself seated in the lobby of a walk-in polyclinic at which he was motioned to a cubicle by a dumpy Atropos in deathly scrubs who, in a twinkling, fastened a tourniquet around his arm before piercing his skin to draw off his vital fluid into a vacutainer tube. The return of this Atropos was not as quick as The Nomad had hoped it would be, and until she reappeared, he was like a cat on a hot tin roof. Then, unfeelingly—perhaps she was just thoroughly adroit in the art of feigning unconcern—she uttered the spiny words tersely; 'you are positive,' which The Nomad seemed to have dreaded to the bone. Unconvinced, The Nomad rapped out the question; 'you mean the virus?' and the Atropos nodded affirmatively, precipitating his head crashing suddenly into his palms. A masculine voice—altogether unendurable and emitted sotto voce—suddenly encouraged The Nomad to rouse his head as he signed to him to check out a plump-looking woman, about four yards away who, according to the gibbous-eyed creature, had been living with the virus for eleven years. Standing almost erect with a slightly hunched back, a rectangular mossy card visible on her left hand, she was juggling a baby in her right arm and seemed to have long-accepted the fate she had been dealt, albeit longing for the possible. Almost involuntarily The Nomad quivered with an expression of disgust that left his face in fragments of scorn, then pity, then hope.

In a different foreground, The Nomad felt marooned and on tenterhooks in a purgatorial realm, his heartbeat sinking like a juddering aircraft in troposphere—until, all of a sudden, he encountered a silvery-haired psychopomp shrouded in a sequinned nacreous vesture, determined, it would seem, to shepherd his atman through the mysterious terra incognita. Unable to read the runes of his sudden pilgrimage through this interminable blankness, his anxiety-ridden heart began to dread his approaching extinction.

Suddenly, his entire being was submerged in the head-splitting sonority of an hourglass-metronome orrery, abruptly interrupted by a series of free-flowing trapezes illuminated by cosmic floodlights which, before long, was rudely transpierced by a psychedelic scrubland which ruptured into view from a mystic diffraction, interminably girded by lateritic dry stone walling, and bespeckled by the yard with what began to shape up in succession as vaudevillian renditions.

From this foreground, a straggling savannah inlaid with a running runlet extrudes in full view with a cockaded buskin-shod coachman steering a hack at a gallop towards unrelieved blankness. And at once following in view was a cavalier knight-errant in full fig seemingly giving chase to the hack, only to be followed at a lick by skulks of civet-hued foxes and a drove of dendritic moose equally giving chase but seemed to be on a hiding to nothing. They were promptly followed in large numbers by a passel of unfledged birdlings in open aviaries, guyed to an invisible shuffler and on the verge of being swallowed holus-bolus by a dusky viper. Then came a brief period of absolute voidness—but not for long, as a fresh foreground sprang up showing fossorial badgers burrowing into clumps of tussocks along the re-emerging maquis—until an unseen tocsin went off suddenly, at which point, the hourglass-metronome orrery regained a dreadful vigour, jangling balefully as though heralding the arrival of a wicked psychopomp, this time awaiting the sands of time to wind up and expedite the unavoidable metronome-induced quietus—the precursor to The Nomad's rigor mortis and ossification in a pallid ossuary.

But just at that very moment, a ventriloquial voice was unexpectedly infused into The Nomad's vision, reciting the exact words of Steinlauf to Primo Levi as it trailed away softly: '… even in this place one can survive, and therefore one must want to survive, to tell the story, to bear witness.'

••••

By and by, The Nomad's bleary eyes could only descry an emerging finch-like background, colourful in scope and glowy in tone, glimmering in tinctures of magenta, mulberry and deep ultramarine. He was at first unsure if his transitional state was unfolding appropriately; the tricoloured tints he was descrying in bits rose in sharp contrast to the ultrapure cotton graveclothes he was expecting to see at the end of the hourglass-metronome lysis. As his cockeyed sight began to evolve clearer, he began to discern Iwa, a truly marvellous nymph, sitting on the downy armchair in an upright posture, tinkering winsomely with a pincushion on her dog-eared paperback, and teasing her cat on the shag rug at the same time. The unaffected dexterity with which she caressed her feline companion and simultaneously occupied her own mind enthralled him somewhat. And the way the cat responded to her motherly touch and the playful cadence of her voice, resulting in a gleeful dancing and spinning—now into the open, now away from view—aroused in him a sense of an almost unnatural and, in fact, a very brief ripple of satisfaction.

Like a flash, their eyes locked out of a clear sky and The Nomad, in his first mero-crystalline sighting of Iwa, was radically smitten with her like one who had slurped a custom-made philtre. Iwa, clothed in her cashmere ochre-poncho, flared crepe pants and suede mule—her pomaded chocolate hair drooping down her shoulders in slick bubble pigtails, her oval-featured cast glimmering endearingly like the baubles on her nose studs, and her deportment instinct with faultless elegance—was to The Nomad all the sign he needed to confirm that he was back among living beings. In time, he became clear-eyed, though with a somewhat peaky aspect, and could not help but regard Iwa as a finely cut gem of perfection honed by the sharpest whetstone a novaculite ever made.

9

As for Iwa, The Nomad was a kindred soul floundering with reason in the black pit of existence, a negatory paragon of unwanted world-weariness, a refuter of afflictive anathemas, an embrocation to the sharp pangs of beingness, a lavation of accompaniment in the vale of heightened lonesomeness—in short he was many a thing her mind could conceive. In the main, she felt drawn to The Nomad far more than she had anyone else in the livelong twenty-four years of her existence. However else he might have disdained life mattered little to her; none was ever as compelling as his most recent attempt to reprehend the tyranny of finality, she thought, regardless of the motivation or circumstance. *None of us would remain in this cheerless place if paradise were known*, she would sometimes say to herself—and The Nomad seemed to have vindicated her when she least expected.

To Iwa, life in Ayé[6] was a mere objectification of valuelessness: It amounted to nothing but a peacockish ruler exulting in The Great Wastage, which was existence itself. And this was why she tried once but failed to end it all, even though Baba Faleke

---

6   The earth.

offered up Ipese, a peculiar sacrifice, consisting mainly of a duck, she-goat, mudfish, and cockerel to mollify and ward off what he described to his acolytes as the turbulent forces of supernatural and psychopathological affliction. But this was not the whole truth. Now privy to the riddles of Ifá or the oracle, Baba Faleke knew that this Ipese, offered before dawn at every full moon, was simply a stopgap to appease the wrath of Èsù, whose wardenship over the crossroads of the in-between world helped to keep the wandering spirit of Iwa's mother at bay. The poor woman, then in her late twenties while Iwa was barely nine, had met a sudden death to which no one could proffer an explanation, leaving her trapped between two worlds—the world of the living and the dead, of the seen and the unseen. In a nutshell, the morbid proclivities evident in Iwa were linked to her ìpín or destiny, which was to either return to the other world and provide companionship to her mother's agitated soul, or in the soonest possible time, open her womb for her mother's soul to nest and define the form of her child before coming into the world of the living. The latter option, despite its salutariness, would wholly depend on Iwa. Baba Faleke, though determined to see his daughter zestful and unbothered by the melancholy and restlessness of the in-between world, was unwilling to deprive her of the choice to choose her partner. Hence, he must continue to offer Ipese to Èsù until Iwa finds someone after her own heart.

Looking into his eyes now, just as he had been looking into hers since he regained consciousness, she felt their unvoiced feelings darting through their shared medium of telepathic *coup de foudre*. As a radical act of disarticulation, the attempt at self-freeing—albeit in the trippiest somnambulistic state imaginable—had united them in a way no other experience this side of the grave ever would have.

'I'm sorry,' The Nomad broke the silence, 'but where am I and how did I get here?'

Right. Now you know to ask.

'I am also curious to know how *you* got here,' she responded in a pouty manner.

Oh. She is a playful one with a sweet-sounding voice.

'Well,' said The Nomad as he trundled to a sedentary posture, still a bit out of sorts, 'all I can remember now is that I was...' then he faltered, looking indecisively at Iwa's countenance...

'Don't worry. This is a safe space,' she said, noticing his hesitance.

'The bottom line is,' he continued, 'I was at a strip club with an acquaintance and we had some drinks... and some heady strain of tea that I learned was from the Great White North. Apparently, it wrecked me with the force of a squall; definitely something I had never experienced before. Uhm— How long was I out?'

'Three days and six hours, I think,' she said, as she peeped into her self-winding, gold-rimmed timepiece.

'Wow.'

'Yeah.'

'Was it deliberate?' she asked, suddenly.

'You mean?'

'The attempt to get so trippy; was it... an extreme escapist's indulgence?'

For a while, he was silent. Then, feeling his back, he let out a sharp grunt.

'I don't know,' he responded gruffly.

'Err… surely, you can give me more?'

'Perhaps. May I know your name?'

'Ah, I thought you'd never ask. My name is Ìwàòlópin, but you may call me Ìwà.'

'Ìwàòlópin… that's a beautiful name,' he drawled fancily.

'Well?'

'What?'

'Won't you tell me your name?'

'I'm Lanre Atiba.'

'Really? Then, it's safe to say we are spun from the same wool?'

'Just so.'

'Water?'

'Yes, please.'

'Generations ago,' she said, as she poured out some water from a pitcher, 'my family moved here from Audoghast to protect our line from the stifling hostility of the Abrahamic religions against our ancestral way of life. Following and practising the teachings of Ifá has been my family's calling for a very long time. But the invaders and expansionists couldn't care less about that. My great grandfather, may his soul rest in peace, was already in his declining years then and nearly did not survive the long, high-risk journey. But as chance would have it, they made it here and became known in time across Kangaba, and even beyond. I was born here and I have never been to Audoghast.'

'Better safe than sorry, trust me,' he said with a wry grimace.

'Are you okay? You seem to be feeling your back often.'

'Um, I think it's lumbago.'

'Okay. We'll make you something for relief. How about some food?'

'I'd appreciate that.'

'And,' he said suddenly as she made to leave the room, causing her to cock her head again in his direction.

'I think… you are right. I should have been more careful, had I not secretly wished to throw caution to the wind and damn the sneering of consequences; you know, to follow the primrose path.'

'I am sure. But hold that thought awhile; I will be back soon. In the meanwhile, feel free to help yourself to a bath. The bathroom is in that corner, and that jute bag has some clothes that should fit.' She said, as she made a beeline for the kitchen.

As he made his way to the bathroom, he surrendered to the vitalizing ambience of the room in which he found himself, impressed with its stark variance in comparison with his squalid place in Niani. He went from observing the damask valance sheet, billowy painting and stylish mod cons to admiring the windowsill, which was bursting with colourful variants of lantanas and heathers and the fenestrate leaves of the rare monstera obliqua lapped over the edges of fluted planters, gleaming almost in tune with wafts of twilight breeze, gently licking the leeward side of the glass, as two or three birds flapped their wings in jig time out of sight. For a while, he stood by the casement, taking in everything.

On her return, conveying a vial of liniment and a trayful of the special cuisine she had personally made for The Nomad, alongside her father, whose transports of joy radiated through his contagious aura, she set his gingerly spiced Asaro and Ogufe before him and watched as he masticated the ambrosia with manly gusto and unspoken derision for Niani's slumgullion, until his last bite.

The Nomad was glad to see the countenance of Baba Faleke, robed in a snowy sacerdotal garment with a tasselled mantle covering his shoulders, and shod in flatform clodhoppers; he had expected a crusted hidebound strait-laced figure. But, far from that, the old man's buoyant disposition and remarkable magnetism leavened the atmosphere of the room.

'Please, don't bother,' said Baba Faleke to The Nomad, who had sprung up to pay obeisance to the good man who saved his life.

'I am very grateful, sir.'

'It's okay. The one to thank is Olodumare, who has granted our supplication that you should live. And thank Ìwàòlópin, too, for unreservedly attending to you while you were temporarily in the other world. If I may ask, is there anyone you would like us to reach out to on your behalf?'

'Ah, no sir. There is none for now.'

'Well, if that is your wish, we will abide by it. But do not hesitate to let us know once you are ready to get in touch with friends or family.'

'Certainly, sir. Thank you very much.'

'I must attend to some visitors now, but feel free to ask Iwa if you need anything.'

'I have been thinking,' said The Nomad to Iwa, following Baba Faleke's exit, 'if you'd pardon my forwardness... is there, perhaps, a reason you have been as concerned as you have about my recovery since I got here?' he asked. And, unsatisfied with his manner of posing the question, he added, 'don't get me wrong, please, as I am very grateful that you have shown me such kindness; but I can't help but wonder that it seems you have other people around who could have attended to me if you wanted.'

'That's true. But, quite a lot happened when you got here, which caused our home to be seized by the urgency that your presence demanded; and though my tending to you was not at all planned in advance, it was not entirely an accident either. In fact, the shortest answer to your question is that I wanted to be here, to see for myself.'

Then, she gently unwrapped the poultice from the ashy delicate she had placed on the side table and offered it to The Nomad.

'It will help with your lumbago,' she added.

'I am grateful for this,' he said, and without biting back, continued 'although, I thought you were going to help me with it since I can't really do it myself,' he said with a ludic air, causing her eyes to split wide like saucers.

'Hmm, I see you are quite bold.'

'The first thing I would like to say,' she said glacially, after tossing The Nomad's pinstriped shirt on the armchair and as she applied the poultice to his lower back, 'is that I have sought to free myself once in the past, although I was neither trippy nor somnambulant like you were.'

'Oh! Do you mind if I ask why?'

'Argh…' she shuddered, then continued, 'must there always be a tangible reason for such a thing? Is the fact itself not an indictment of the inanity of reason? Should it not be that the "why" loses its prestige when disregarded by the singular esteem of the deed?' The silence that followed dragged for a few seconds before she continued:

'And, as to your initial question: I think it was because I instantly identified with your courage, the courage to trust— even when out of touch with the material world—the sublimity of topping oneself, which was also what I felt during my previous attempt. How certain I am now that the one who commits the act is an aesthete. Such courage! Such disdain! Such indifference to the elusiveness all around us! I have found that there is no formidable reason in this world—once you dismiss the fear of the imaginary—that could invalidate the splendid appeal of it—and it is this absence of reason, interestingly, that animates me.' She concluded, leaving The Nomad buried in quietness for a short time.

'This courage you speak of,' he finally began to respond, 'though I am not sure I would have had it were I sober, reinforces my recent suspicion, so to speak, that the ultimate fruition of life may as well be death. But I do imagine and query myself, sometimes, that why rush it, if, in the end, it is ineludible?'

'And who determines if it has been rushed or not? If, as you suggest, death is the ultimate fruition, with whom lies the prerogative of an appropriate time?'

'Right, I think you have a point,' he said, as he cocked his head in his prostrate position towards Iwa who was now flanking him in a seated posture on the bed. Then he continued, 'at bottom, time is as relative as it is universal, never quite this nor completely that, and I guess its interpretation should—if it be nothing else—be always tempered by that fact.'

Now, seeming to be suddenly overtaken by some curious scheme, The Nomad continued, 'but, imagine that life were some kind of hawser that enjoys the privilege of mooring only when a barque, which in this case would be the will to survive, finds such appealing inanity—as you say—which may be said to be adequate for wanting to be moored… what would yours be?'

'Hmm, you ask a tricky but very good question. For me, such appealing inanity would be the wish to be understood.'

'In that case,' said he, 'try me.'

She paused for a while, shook her head knowingly from one side to another, then responded, 'I have just one question: how did we get here? I feel like I have just been wheedled into playing hopscotch without my consent... Like Sidi in Baroka's sleeping quarters.'

Instantly, an unfeigned spell of mirth erupted between the duo, travelling now and then to the ears of Baba Faleke, his acolytes and his departing pilgrims in wavelets of gamesomeness, and lasted awhile into the bargain as The Nomad and Iwa regaled each other with memorable childhood stories.

'Well, I guess if you know Sidi and Baroka, then you must know Ali and Simbi?'

'Of course, I do. Bless my father's undaunted heart for making sure I didn't miss out on those classic treasures. Oh, I remember those days when he would take his time to speak to me about their importance, about how we must never forget the ways of our people, how he wants me to continue to experience Audoghast from outside Audoghast. Anyhow, here is your proof: "This is Ali. Ali is Simbi's brother. Look at him. What is he doing? He is cutting the grass..."'

'Hahaha... Encore! How about Mr Nwosu and his two daughters and four sons?'

'Yes! And do you remember The Joys of Motherhood, Sugar Girl, Things Falls Apart, and Alawiye?'

'I remember them all. And... Edet lives in Calabar!'

'Oh my days, that was a favourite, you know. Do you remember the text?'

'Of course,' he said, proceeding confidently to recite the famous passage, '"Edet lives in Calabar, he is eight years old…"' then they began to reel off the passage, as their voices trailed away… '"every morning he goes to school, but in the afternoon he stays at home…"'

And so their voices diminuendoed as the cast of fleece clouds yielded in shifting mass to the force of convection, and the undulation of fibrous matter became billows of shrouded vapour, accelerating tropospheric cumulonimbus and galvanizing the wind into a roving force of nature to which the trees joggled and flocks of avifauna flapped about like a shot, twittering to the glory of natural phenomena. Soon, sunlight vanished into the horizon as the rumbling of melting thunder crashed against the deterrent carapace impeding the fluttering butterflies of primal intimacy, sweltering between The Nomad and Iwa.

Before long, a shaft of twilight from Osumare, the rainbow deity, flashed across the babbling ripples of the lake as an arched spectrum of glittering coruscation, intent on inverting the order of heavenly and earthly expressions. Then, as precipitation condensed into masses of water droplets in defiance of unrelieved entrapment in the pitchy cloudscape, driblets and drizzles pierced the towering blanket until vigorous sleets and cloudbursts descended at once on the surface of the earth, lashing against the final husks of temperance in defence of passionate overtones blaring through the skies, tippling down with the flavour of erotic *pas de deux*, to The Nomad's exertion of the lead in his pencil, and the amorous consummation of this peculiar *coup de foudre*.

'Is Iwa still with our guest?' asked Baba Faleke, as Fagbami swiftly responded in the affirmative.

Seated under the skillion where his guests had just consulted him on a private concern, his geomantic divination board on the centre stool of the deck reflecting thoughtfulness and divine inspiration, Baba Faleke looked out to the sky, unmindful of the tireless cataract and ice pellets; his refined demeanour evincing the serenity of certainty, his ruminant form saturated with mystical veneration. And, in his wonted sacerdotal fashion, he began to recite the words of Eji Ogbe, 'the moist air of consciousness,' in one of its gnomic verses:

'oju ko kan mi
emi ko kan ju
ni o difa fun Ero Pese
Ti o nlo se oko Igbin
Igbin nwa oko
Ero Pese nwa iyawo
Awon mejeeji wa lo si ile alawo ni otooto
Ero pese wa bere lowo ifa wipe nje oun le ni aya
Igbin naa bere lowo alawo re wipe nje oun le ni oko
Awon babalawo awon mejeeji so fun won wipe,
Ki won lo rubo ki won si tun lo ni opolopo suuru
Wipe ati oko ati aya yio pade ara won
Bayi ni olukaluku won ba lo ru ebo ti babalawo won ka fun won
Nitori ototo ni won lo si ile alawo
Ti o si je odu kan naa ni o yo fun awon mejeeji lai mo ara won ri
Bi won se rubo tan ni Ero Pese pade Igbin
Ni won ba soro ti oro won ye ara won,
Ti won wa gbe ara won ni iyawo
Ni nkan won ba bere si ni dara si,

Ti oro won ba dero ti ayo idunnu owo,
alafia ati ire gbogbo bere si ni to won lowo
ni won wa njo ni won wa nyo'[7]

Translation:
I am in no haste
I am in no race
Divined Ifá for Tranquillity
The soon-to-be husband to The Snail
The Snail craved a husband
Tranquillity craved a fitting wife
Separately, they approached different Ifá diviners
Tranquillity sought to know if he would find a wife
The Snail, also, sought to know if she would find a husband
Both seekers were thus instructed,
To offer sacrifices and imbibe bountiful patience
That the seekers would both find each other
And each went their way to offer their sacrifices
For they had consulted Ifá separately
Yet the same Odu had emerged for both, though unacquainted
Thus Tranquillity and The Snail encountered each other
     just after their sacrifices
And became smitten with each other hence,
And became man and wife
And became prosperous in all things,
Flourishing in ease, gladness and means,
Bursting with health and successfulness,
And forever basking in bliss

---

7   (Frisvold, 2016)

10

It was now exactly fifteen months since The Nomad was piggybacked to Ile Ayo, and fifty-one to the day since nomadism became his lot. He was now a dutiful husband to Iwa, a filial son to Baba Faleke, a farmer in his own right, and together with Iwa, was expecting the patter of tiny feet in less than a month.

He got married to Iwa in a very modest nuptials (prompted by one of Baba Faleke's divinatory mediumship with Ela, the witness to Fate, and the oracle that The Nomad and Iwa's fates forbade any boisterous celebration), which his mother, his only living parent with whom he had an undefined bond, gleefully attended from Audoghast. But his former landlady's son, Johnson—who was as right as rain and never deliriant after the night at Kangaba Lounge—having watched his mother cross the divide after battling coronary thrombosis, had given up all they had in Niani and left Kangaba altogether.

His diurnal routine since his nuptials had been from Ile Ayo to Baba Faleke's ten and a half hectares arable and sheep farm where he would toil with genius and brawn thrice or so a week, diligently attending to the flocks, staving off overgrazing, infestation, and watching out for general health troubles from pen to pasturage and vice versa. Occasionally, he would lend a hand to random and methodical enterprises related to Baba Faleke's divine line of country. And by all appearances, The Nomad's daily activities, both in regard to the farm and his duties as a husband to Iwa, had been conducted without a blot on his escutcheon. He spared no effort in ensuring that the fruitage, livestock, various crops, particularly the vegetables and amaranths, and profits on vendible products from the farm were conscientiously husbanded and accounted for. He was thoroughly adored by his wife who had become a greengrocer of note and relied partly on his toil on the farm, and fondly cherished by Baba Faleke, so much so that he was promptly held in high esteem by many of their neighbours in Cannah, notwithstanding his being held in derision as a rootless parvenu by those who were green with envy, for whom he did not care two hoots.

From time to time, The Nomad would sit and pally with Baba Faleke at the veranda, discussing politics, society and religion, and sometimes just shooting the breeze while imbibing draughts of the old critter's favourite premium flagon cider. There were times, also, when both men would regale each other, sometimes in the presence of Baba Faleke's acolytes, with their knowledge of Ifá's many-sided theogonies, which The Nomad had been learning unflaggingly and of which he had since found Èsù to be his favourite deity. And even though he never became a dyed-in-the-wool Ifá religioner, for he had over the years become religionless, Baba Faleke never took his irreligious stance amiss and embraced him no less, and even encouraged him to always make no bones about his convictions, be it on religion or any other matter.

Some of The Nomad's favourite memories came from the special log-fire nights when they would all assemble as a family at Ile Ayo's forecourt and sit by the fireside shaded by bosky canopies and moonlight, without a tincture of electricity—often disconnected on purpose to gratify the household's folkloric sensibilities—and learn the art and verses of infant eulogium, for which Iwa was always the unrivalled tutor; and revel—sometimes carousing, high-fiving and doubling over in transports of side-splitting legends and anecdotes.

Having intimated the household with the facts and circumstances of his becoming a nomad, including the gory bits of the Southern Audoghast demonstration and the consequential decree of the Audoghast Police Force, which precipitated his flight and aggrieved him to the utmost degree—including, at the same time, how he had also heard on the grapevine that Ìgè had been injected with a morbid substance that would quicken his meeting his end, whether within or outside the pen—so that, in the end, The Nomad was all too willing to solemnly renounce his connection to Audoghast, though he would sometimes groan inwardly that he could no longer claim his roots as he'd love to—leading him, all the same, to implicitly settle into his self-assertive identity as a man, a rootless nomad, a son, a husband, and a farmer at Ile Ayo.

More than anything else, The Nomad and Iwa had a flawless relationship that evinced their determination to take the plunge for their union, brooking neither spiteful division nor being as cross as two sticks with each other, complementing their propensities to existential fatigue and self-freeing like a knife through butter, sometimes even shrouding themselves in mantles of self-transcendence. They basked in the certitude of being to each other an unswerving bastion of dependability; the one, his roving eye shut, being an incorrigible fortification in times of mental torpor, and the other, her vestal purity to her beholder unflawed, being a real trooper in times of desolation.

The most looked-for moments of the week by Iwa and The Nomad were the private nights *à deux* when neither of the couple was bogged down by the day's leadenness, when the one was ensheathed in the other's arms in their interior-sprung matrimonial bed, crooning in dulcet tunes of conjugal delights, indulging their sensual whims and snogging in the sanctuary of intramural plants, alive and flourishing by virtue of Iwa's green fingers. And there were days, much too often to track, when The Nomad would lay in bed with Iwa, burbling euphonious rhymes to his seed protruding in her belly, sometimes even having a go at prestidigitation supposedly to divert the unborn child, always assuming it would be a boy and constantly calling it Lánléhìn, in honour of his friend who had fallen at the barricades.

'Hey big man, daddy's name for you is Lánléhìn,' he would say in whispery tones to his wife's gestative womb. They had unequivocally decided against a sonogram, wanting to preserve the sanctity of the unknown. But once, Iwa had asked: 'what if it's a she?' And The Nomad had told her in a heartbeat: 'then, we will name her Ìwàòlópin.' Iwa, always taking pleasure in her husband's affectionate remarks, giggled and responded that in addition to his preferred name, she would also name the child Àtúnwá[8], in memory of her late mother.

But on one such night, everything changed. It was, in fact, a wee before the crack of dawn, when Iwa, enrobed in her bedtime cotton-lace bustier, which to the couple was a

---

8   Rebirth.

particular favourite, and fast asleep in the crook of her husband's arm, when the latter suddenly awoke as if to a reveille, feeling interiorly peculiar, and tilted her sidewards, making sure she was as snug as a bug. Seated and his head reclined against the headboard, his eyes suddenly became rheumy, and a wave of impulsion stirred him to his feet. He leaned towards his wife and planted a doting kiss on her cheek, then turned about and tucked a few accoutrements in his mud-coloured rucksack.

In jig time, he slipped into his dun-coloured worsted checked shirt, inky flannel jeans and retro sneakers, running his fingers briefly across his chin-curtain beard as he donned his crocheted gingham trilby. And then, one last time, he cast a side glance on the spellbinder, which was Iwa, and bobbed his head as if completely certain she was the perfect woman any man could hope to have in his corner.

Outside, pausing briefly to soak up the dewy mustiness, a cryptic smile sown with intrigue creased his shaggy-browed dial, as he soaked himself in the matin of warbling birds and the thrill of newness. And, having zilch idea of his next stop or even destination, yet bursting with conation that he was on the right tram, he beetled off thinking that he was again a nomad to the bone. 'Sometimes,' he mused to himself, 'you have to shut an eye to see your nose better.'

A Legacy of Negro Nihilism

My grandmother has narrated this story to me again and again, often making me revisit it in my mind and my soliloquies, so much so that I might even be accused of being too saccharine in my approbation of the story. Be that as it may, I am convinced that this story deserves to be told to the wider world, for it has, for long enough, been a caviar to the general.

For some time now, the wicker chair at the centre of Oloye Todun's spiderwebbed verandah has shrouded itself in legendary repute. It was on this chair that Oloye's willowy pendant, a family heirloom, was found the day after she proclaimed her contentious credo.

On that epoch-making day, redolent with earthly rigour and curdled fervour, there was something clutching at Oloye's pharynx, a sweltering so oppressive and spiny she could not but yield, at long last, to its compulsive leadenness. The matter had been on her mind long enough; her very existence had become, at that point, only too steeped in her thematic thrust, so that she could not but regale her audience with what had become a self-consuming preoccupation. It was, after all—as she would later admit to my grandmother that night—a fated self-confession. "Samira, this is a turn I must take to calm the gales in my belly," Oloye had stated solemnly, referring to the disquietude which had somewhat eclipsed her existence. Samira, now my raddled nonagenarian grandmother, acquiesced quietly. She has been a fabulous griot in Heathland since her salad days, and in addition to mythmaking and oratory, she was perfectly versed in reading the room.

Oloye was the fourth of her mother's children. She belonged to a maternal descent line of teenage Africans who had been snatched off the trading markets of the Western Sudan and shipped away in Portuguese caravels, the ropy gris-gris around their ankles notwithstanding, only to become parents and nurturers of hundreds, even thousands of Mulattoes in the West Indies. At age sixteen when her mother succumbed to consumption—like her own mother before her after harrowing years on cotton plantations, leaving behind an indeterminate worth of effects and the family's lavaliere that somehow survived that horrendous transatlantic voyage, Oloye had pulled herself up by her bootstraps and, later, dedicated the full treatment to her decade-long spell in what was then called the Sustainable Development sector, where she gained some standing for keeping the bastards honest and more. Yet, all the comforts and self-righteousness that came with that world were, alas, not enough to smother the inadequacies aflame in Oloye, not even the feeling that she was merely a handy tool in the thraldom of a ruthless and agonizing hegemonic force, unwittingly abetting a cause that did not belong to her. But a chance public encounter with Samira had given her the clarity she yearned for, and though her self-transformation had required a capital effort to come to, she was, in due course, imbued with a thoroughly dignifying sense of liberty that severed her from the yoke of her past.

Heathland, however, underwent a total sea change which reduced it to such badlands where public safety and social services were clamant needs banished to the imaginary, even as Macoute and his sinecures dug their noses in the trough. Now at the rostrum facing a devoted audience, Oloye felt possessed by the impassioned gods of oration. The audience, some of whom my grandmother had assumed would never in this world understand Oloye's sometimes involuted turn of phrase, had been both startled and captivated by her uncanny phraseology.

'The topic of my speech today,' she had said, in her typical imperial mannerism, 'is Negro Nihilism.'

It was not *nihilism*—even though some of her listeners had no knowledge of the signification of the word, and had conveniently flung it to the slag of novel words that Oloye sometimes used, to enthral her listeners and admirers—that startled the audience. It was, rather, that sacrilegious word *Negro* that had startled her usually receptive crowd. Many of Oloye's peers had sworn off the word altogether, primarily to avoid the arctic backlash of the radical chic—and one might be right to assume that even the cockiest funambulist would have dodged the word. But Oloye didn't.

My grandmother would later tell me that though she too had been a bit taken aback, she had merely shrugged and assumed on the spot, that only a rapid flush of Negroized emotion would traverse the countenance of Oloye's multiracial audience. But she was wrong: the word became the essence of all that Oloye said and withheld; it became the air that the audience breathed and the streamer of the papers and free sheets, affecting a dragging reverberation that, no matter what, just won't be dispelled, even long after the event.

Of the whole audience, my grandmother said it was the pair of one fizzy Danielle, a native of Heathland who had then just returned home from the British Isles with a plum in her mouth, and Miguel, a prissy self-avowed poetaster originally from the Orinoco plains in Venezuela, that mainly seemed to have felt the masses of that Negroized surge. The way I understood it was that the pair probably personified the attendant facial contortion that the word *Negro* dutifully summoned whenever it spurted from a stubborn cakehole, transmuting in affective cast from repulsive to forbearing, depending on the racial stamp of its agent.

Because it was the elegant and robustious Oloye who used the word, it seemed to have been, to an extent, cloaked with a particularly unexplainable grimace, limp and shorn of bile, by the audience. She had, after all, niched herself within the realm of Heathland's celebrity sainthood as a speechmaker of universal distinction—although to the displeasure of her early detractors who would later dismiss their own detraction as merely figmental—by often plucking acrid fruits from one controversial tree to another, riding on the ephemeral crosswind of public drama or creating one herself. Like when she said, without rhyme or reason, that the politicians in Heathland ought to be gathered in one room and clinically shot in the head, insisting that they were always going to be a viper in the bosom of Heathlanders. (Even now, my grandmother would sometimes say she agreed with that controversial opinion of Oloye, saying the only challenge was the execution, or the details of it).

Or when Oloye said she would renounce her Heathland citizenship if what she described as *the canker of transgenderism* was ever decreed into the statute book of Heathland. In those days, it was the norm under the regime of Macoute, Heathland's infamous dictator and deep-dyed westernizer, to decree into law anything from the Occident. The marrow of Oloye's gusty opposition to transgenderism—as my grandmother would sometimes zestfully narrate to me as if this bit of the story suddenly became anew when retold—was that it is unhistorical to Heathland and that it is a noxious seed that Heathland must keep at bay, far away from the caricatural appetite of Heathland's sophisticates. And so for a good while, Oloye persisted in her antitransgender standpoint, insisting now and then that she was neither transphobic nor troglodytic as her virulent detractors labelled her, that she only wanted sanity.

By and by, Oloye outgunned her detractors and grew—by her own adroitness in managing and benefitting from knotty controversies—in popularity, gelt and authority. Her speeches, too, underwent a perpetual flux of refinement, getting bolder and more unequivocal in brevity and acerbity, until she became too flawless to be flawed in the hearts and minds of Heathlanders. At that point, Oloye's name had become a household word, always gusting confidently through the wedges separating her from whatsoever household that had yet to get wind of her speechmaking bravura and connecting with them through her elocutionary flair and strength of character.

Unlike several others in her hallowed circle of canonized celebrities—like Father Caritas, the celebrity pastor whose much-advertised donatives consisted only in superabundant trinketry; and Madam Islamia, also known as The Juggernaut, a political éminence grise whose overreaching influence conferred the sanctified turpitude of orchestrating a double bind in any

169

election cycle in Heathland—Oloye did not desperately solicit the common touch; instead, it was a natural out-turn of her outflowing charisma.

Often, my grandmother would say there was just a great deal about Oloye that screamed nonconformism and shrouded her in solid mystique. From the cognomen she chose for herself from the get-go, which is more popular in Heathland with titled personages which she was not, to the outré themes she dilated on periodically, which rattled the cage of Macoute's apparatchiki more than somewhat, so that she was regarded by not a few of them as Beelzebub incarnate. Perhaps it is this redoubtable form of Oloye, her tenacious spirit when confronted with malignant opposition, her resolute moral constitution, and that exceptional facility to bend language to her will, which has made her existence and legacy enthralling despite the dissipation of time. This is a view not solely mine, at least not if Salina, my mother, whose fascination with Oloye is only closely matched by mine, has got anything to say about it. All the same, Oloye's popularity grew by leaps and bounds across the sweeping landform of Heathland. It was at this peak in her speechmaking métier that she hired my grandmother as her personal assistant, and together, according to my grandmother, they rode on a slipstream of Oloye's incalculable renown.

• • • •

And then, something changed about Oloye. It was, at first, understated and unnoticed, occasionally punctuated by flying spells of jollity. Increasingly, however, Oloye would become morose, ruminant and inward-looking, reading this, that, and the other doorstop rigorously, as though she were faithfully observing and becoming habituated to a prescribed procedure of solitudinarian transformation. There would come, also, a tangible world-weariness in her expressions and diurnal somatic motions, a lasting flaccidity that prefigured existential exhaustion, as though she were internally squirming in some obscure, viscous lava flow. She would refuse to make speeches, decline public appearances, and grow testier by the day. Samira, who was then in her early twenties, would, in time, learn to tip-toe around the middle-aged Oloye to avoid becoming the victim of her testy outbursts.

And then, one day, out of the blue, it would seem a further change had descended on Oloye; a gust, perhaps, of epiphany and salutary refraction. The way she moved, gesticulated, and charged my grandmother with such and such detail effused a peculiar certitude, a resoluteness that was as stimulative as it was questionable. It was as if her concrete ground down until that point had suddenly evaporated into a cloud wrack.

On this account, Oloye declared a few days later her intention to host one more event that would be her swansong, her last formal speech as a speechmaker, which she decided would be an out-by gathering at a fitting agora in Heathland, consisting not only of native Heathlanders but also her wide-ranging interracial followers; and which, in her customary fashion, would be a concourse of persons from all social strata.

• • • •

This was the event that Danielle and Miguel would attend and become the personification of unspoken emotions. But Oloye was deliberately inattentive to their affected reactions, proceeding to deliver her speech exactly as she had intended:

Let me start by saying I have included *Negro* in my theme, though I know it is a jaundiced word, because I wish for all of us here to transcend, if only for this moment, the chastening simplism of that word. Being a mulatto of mixed paisano parentage, I have only recently begun to reappraise my identity as it is and the contextual source of our individual and multiracial identities.

As you all know, I have declined to speak publicly for a while, and during my self-imposed absence, I have come to realize, in virtue of what I believe is the life-changing epiphany I have experienced, that we have left too many questions unanswered in our time. In short, we have failed— in the same sense as the majority of those before us—to emulate the drawdown from historicity which a miniscule lot of those before us did quite assiduously. For instance, popular understanding of our history is that our forebears had suffered a great injustice, had been deracinated or displaced forcibly, had laboured intensely, had been bastinadoed unjustly and mistreated inhumanely, all of which is true, and which makes our blood congeal, sometimes with fright and other times the craving for retribution.

From the Lost Times to Neanderthal Man, from the civilizations of the Nile to Mesopotamia, from the Metal Age of the Blackamoor south of the Sahara to Negritude, from cold-blooded dogmas to tranquillizing idealisms, from the Middle Passage to abolitionists and revolutionists, we have witnessed what we have repeatedly described as a change— credited, of course, to the relentless zeal of equalitarian apostles and rebels—a vincular progression, as we like to say, from the godawful to the sanguine.

But what we construe as change, in short, is a misconstruction of chameleonic condescension. So if, as in my case and that of countless others, one is a product of situational ancestry, and one's father happened to have loved one's mother no more than a slaveholder loved his slave or a houndmaster loved his hound; but, in virtue of universal and structural chameleonic condescension, one manages to 'get on' despite one's afflictive heritage—not so much as to be completely severed from that heritage in material experience, but enough to not have to directly be a slave or a hound—we call it change. Never mind that a veneered denial is the plank of these equalitarian concessions by the condescending, that the weight of forcible deracination is intergenerationally afflictive, or that the identity of the afflicted is unchanged, perhaps even ineradicable now. Yet we continue to call it change—that anodyne word we often use to palliate our long-drawn-out decomposition.

As a consequence, our understanding of change is every whit far from a hard-boiled construal of the word: that is, it is not whole. Our understanding of change is a mere repetition of compelling realities, responsibilities, principal instincts, and principal actors from one to another; it is not—which it should be—an embodiment of something tangible and total, new and striking, stimulating and also humbling. So it is not change because it is not a binary singularity, or at the very least, a singularity of consistent moieties.

And because this change is now non-existent, we crash into parallelism, comparing and contrasting now with before, a nostalgic intercommunication between where we are now and our distant past, torn between the unfathomable

173

beginning and the inconceivable end, ferreting around temporal antipodes for something more concrete, something not as impure as our present, an indication of a future that is more sanguine; we keep mimeographing, fabricating and ascribing to the past what we think belongs to it. Gone are the days when we proudly declaimed that we would ride on past glories, stomp on current victories, and emerge unvanquished. All our struggles symbolize a frantic jostle towards Provenance, an enduring appeal to return to the beginning even if it means vanishing, to re-enact now the things that once belonged to the past. But we are unable, ultimately, to confront the sterility of this paradisal obsession, our obsession with Provenance and the First Cause, something on which to hinge our realities and expectations, to give change a compelling signification, and equalitarianism a realistic touch.

Ages unknown from now, some of us will look back and realize we've been duped by time: the sameness of yesterday and today, of tomorrow and later days. And like *Joebell and America*, after failing to game the behemoths of the condescending, we will begin to understand that however great a seafarer one may be, no man walks on water, except in legends and myths. The roads are the same, whether blasted and torturous on this side or galvanized and gilded on the other side. And when we plunge into the mercurial kaleidoscope of J'ouvert, getting lost in our little lickerish marsupia, we still struggle at night to remain impervious to the throes of the insomniac duppy, and at dawn, we still rise to the keening of jumbie birds—the ineluctable presage of our final decomposition.

And when our nostalgia invariably dispraises our melancholy and flings the sterility of our obsession back in our wistful faces; when the condescending fails to realize the privilege of condescension nor the noblesse oblige of its unmerited privilege; when our logic chopping tomes fail to gratify our curiosities; when we realize, ultimately, that we are all unwilling automatisms, entrapped in our rueful state of enfeoffed tenancies; when neither monoculturalism nor multiculturalism is able to overturn our conflicted identities; when the doltishness of sacerdotalist preachments can no longer assuage our existential rage; when, in short, we begin to go stir-crazy courtesy of the unchallenged tyranny of the unseen mailed fist masterminding the stigmata dotting our existences—that is when, I hope, we shall begin to understand the *soul* of Negro Nihilism.

It was the day after this speech—which, by the way, my grandmother insists is irrefragably moot—the whole of Heathland woke up to realize that Oloye Todun had ended it all and left behind her cherished family heirloom on the wicker chair. As to the import of this relic, a great deal of pontification has been proclaimed, but no one really knows. Nonetheless, my grandmother prefers to end this story by saying: whether we like it or not Negro Nihilism is the legacy Oloye bequeathed to the world.

www.ingramcontent.com/pod-product-compliance
Lightning Source LLC
Chambersburg PA
CBHW021221260626
47172CB00002B/547